Runaway

THE OUTSIDER SERIES
BOOK FIVE

LORHAINNE ECKHART

Give feedback on the book at:
lorhainneeckhart@hotmail.com

Twitter: @LEckhart
Facebook: AuthorLorhainneEckhart

Printed in the U.S.A

What reviewers are saying

— *"Another hot Friessen Man. It is a pleasure watching Andy learn how to be a real husband and father."*

REVIEWER, MIRANDA

—*"This definitely proves money doesn't buy love. What a suspenseful love story."*

REVIEWER, APRIL

—*"Loved it !!! Better than the others... This book is one of my favorites of the series. It's a must read series."*

ELIZABETH LOPEZ

—*"I loved this book as much as I loved the ones before. All of the books about the Friessen men are great. Hard to put down. I can't wait for the next one to come out."*

PETRA BYERS

—"I was blown away by this book. Loved it. Was not a huge Andy fan in the beginning but I really do like him now."

LOCABEAR

*The Friessen Family Series
Reading order:*

The Outsider Series

The Forgotten Child (Brad and Emily)
A Baby And A Wedding
Fallen Hero (Andy, Jed, and Diana)
The Awakening (Andy and Laura)
Secrets (Jed and Diana)
Runaway (Andy and Laura)
Overdue
The Unexpected Storm (Neil and Candy)
The Wedding (Neil and Candy)

The Friessens: A New Beginning

The Deadline (Andy and Laura)
The Price to Love (Neil and Candy)
A Different Kind of Love (Brad and Emily)
A Vow of Love, A Friessen Family Christmas

The Friessens

The Reunion
The Bloodline (Andy & Laura)
The Promise (Diana & Jed)
The Business Plan (Neil & Candy)
The Decision (Brad & Emily)
First Love (Katy)
Family First
Leave the Light On
In the Moment
In the Family: A Friessen Family Christmas
In the Silence
In the Stars
In the Charm
Unexpected Consequences
It Was Always You
The First Time I Saw You
Welcome to My Arms
Welcome to Boston (A Paige & Morgan Short Story)
I'll Always Love You
Ground Rules
A Reason to Breathe
You Are My Everything
Anything For You
The Homecoming
When They Were Young (Link included FREE with The
Homecoming)
Stay Away From My Daughter
The Bad Boy
A Place of Our Own
The Visitor
All About Devon
Long Past Dawn
How to Heal a Heart
Keep Me In Your Heart

The Friessen Family

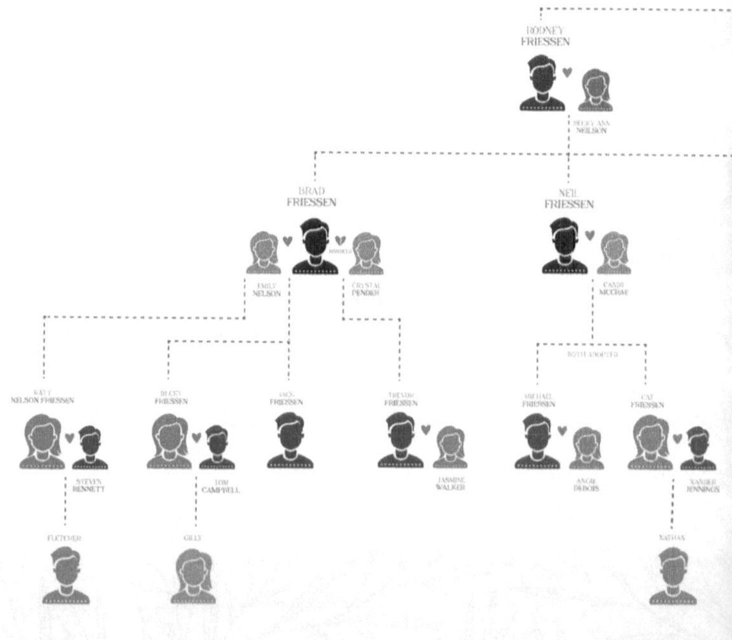

The Outsider Series

THE FORGOTTEN CHILD	BRAD & EMILY
A BABY AND A WEDDING	BRAD & EMILY & and her half Rodney & Becky
FALLEN HERO	JED, DIANA & ANDY
THE SEARCH	JED, DIANA & ANDY
THE AWAKENING	ANDY & LAURA

The Outsider Series

SECRETS	DIANA & JED with the entire Friessen Family
RUNAWAY	ANDY & LAURA
OVERDUE	JED & DIANA
THE UNEXPECTED STORM	NEIL & CANDY
THE WEDDING	NEIL & CANDY and the entire Friessen Family

The Friessens: A New Beginning

THE DEADLINE	ANDY & LAURA
THE PRICE TO LOVE	NEIL & CANDY
A DIFFERENT KIND OF LOVE	BRAD & EMILY
A VOW OF LOVE	THE ENTIRE
A FRIESSEN FAMILY CHRISTMAS	FRIESSEN FAMILY

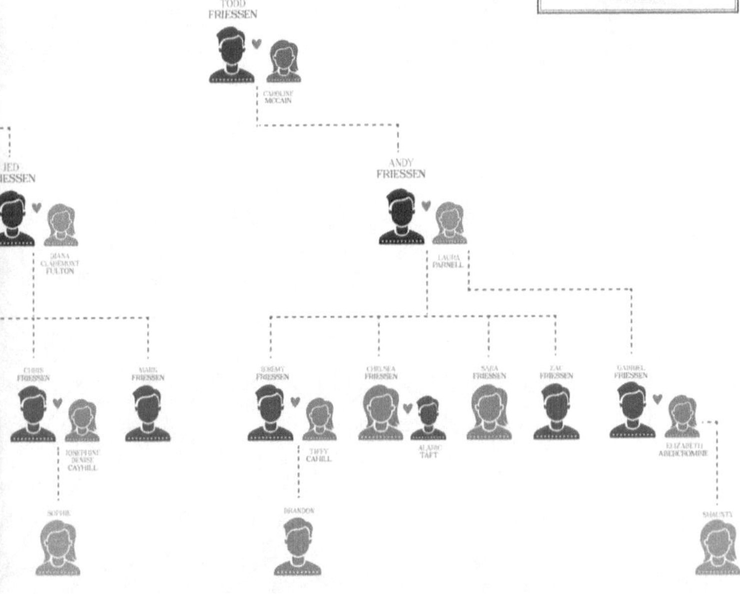

...riessens

THE ENTIRE FRIESSEN FAMILY
ANDY & LAURA
JED & DIANA
NEIL & CANDY
BRAD & EMILY
KATY & STEVEN
KATY & STEVEN

The Friessens

LEAVE THE LIGHT ON	KATY & STEVEN
IN THE MOMENT	BECKY & TOM
IN THE FAMILY, *A Friessen Family Christmas*	THE ENTIRE FRIESSEN FAMILY
IN THE SILENCE	CAT & XANDER
IN THE STARS	DANNY & EVIE
IN THE CHARM	CHRIS & J.D.
UNEXPECTED CONSEQUENCES	CHRIS & J.D.

The Friessens

IT WAS ALWAYS YOU	KATY & STEVEN
THE FIRST TIME I SAW YOU	GABRIEL & ELIZABETH
WELCOME TO MY ARMS	CHELSEA & ALARIC
WELCOME TO BOSTON	PAIGE & MORGAN *A Friessen bonus short story*
I'LL ALWAYS LOVE YOU	JEREMY
GROUND RULES	JEREMY & TIFFY
A REASON TO BREATHE	TREVOR & JASMINE
YOU ARE MY EVERYTHING	MICHAEL & ANGIE
ANYTHING FOR YOU	*A Cat & Candlelight Novella*
THE HOMECOMING	THE ENTIRE FRIESSEN FAMILY

*"**Just when you think the story can't get any hotter, you're sadly mistaken.**"*

Six months ago, Laura walked out on the only man she's ever truly loved. Even though wealthy Andy Friessen has been looking for her what he doesn't know is the secret Laura has been hiding. And when Andy finds out he'll risk everything to get her back.

CHAPTER

One

"Are you Andy Friessen?"

Andy didn't bother to glance up from where he was bent over the hoof, picking mud and gravel from his three-year-old buckskin, Ladystar. Andy dug out the last dried chunk of mud, wanting to snap at whoever was bothering him. "Damn kid I hired didn't clean out her hoof after riding her," he muttered. He put her hoof down, and she stomped and pranced as Andy pressed his hand to her hind quarter. He wiped the sweat from his forehead and picked up her front hoof, starting to dig around the frog, picking out all the dried mud. Bent over as he was, Andy could see a pair of blue jeans on some man who was standing behind his horse. "I wouldn't stand there if I were you," he said, setting down the mare's hoof and standing up. "It's a good way to get yourself kicked."

A short man wearing shades and a tan sports coat stepped sideways around a pile of fresh manure. "I'm looking for Andy Friessen," the man said.

"Yeah, well, you found him. What do you want?" he

snapped, irritated because all he wanted to do was saddle the horse, head onto the trail, and ride for the next few hours without one more person asking him another stupid question. He just wanted some peace.

"You've been served." The man slapped court papers in his hand and then hurried the other way as if Andy was going to chase him down and pound the crap out of him.

"Hey, what the hell is this?" Andy barked at the man now jogging up the driveway.

Andy swore as he flipped open the document and read **_Petition for Divorce_** in bold black letters. Laura was suing him for divorce! He couldn't believe it. Hell, any woman would give her right arm to be married to him, to have his name. As he read on, he felt like ice shards were ripping through his veins as he saw Diana Friessen's name written at the bottom as the lawyer of record. She was his cousin Jed's wife and the one woman he'd probably go to his grave loving. How could she do this to him and not call him? Did Jed know?

He hadn't heard from Laura in over six months. She'd walked out the door without saying goodbye to him, taking her son, Gabriel, with her and leaving everything he'd bought for them behind. Andy had been furious at first. Hell, he'd even tracked her down to where she'd been staying with the old cook, Aida, who still worked for Andy and his family. But Laura had refused to speak with him, and Aida sent him away and asked him not to come back again. Six months ago, he had expected Laura to return home to the estate with her tail tucked between her legs. After all, she had no money, no family, and no resources, with a little boy to feed, clothe, and shelter. She needed him.

But she didn't come back. And she didn't phone.

Then he worried. He'd married her to protect her

when she'd been forced to live in her car after she couldn't pay rent because his mother had fired her when she worked as a maid—all because she'd knocked over a Christmas tree. When the sheriff had found her living in her car, the authorities took Gabriel and stuck him into a foster home that wasn't even fit to care for a dog. Andy had stepped in and married her to help her get Gabriel back. Why had he done it? Because the whole messed-up situation that had spiraled from bad to worse had been his fault.

As Andy read through the black print and legalese, he fought back a rising tide of anger and disbelief. Well, to hell with her. She appreciated nothing he'd done for her. What should he expect from someone so young and ungrateful and...? He stopped cold when an icy chill raced through him as he realized she'd asked for nothing from the divorce, not one red cent from him.

Andy came from one of the wealthiest families in the county; she could easily have asked for a fortune and gotten it even though they'd been married less than a year. Andy knew she wasn't a fool, and deep down he knew she was no gold digger. She was hurt and vulnerable and innocent, and he hadn't treated her with a lick of respect. The fact was that he was having a hard time admitting what a prick he'd been. He was ashamed of the way he'd taken charge of her life, of Gabriel's, without sharing anything of his life with her.

Well, to hell with her. He would just wash his hands of her and say good riddance. He crumpled the papers and went to stuff them in his pocket, then stopped when he glimpsed the back door open. Aida, the old cook, stepped out of the staff entrance of the vast Friessen mansion, carrying her coat and purse, having finished her work for the day.

Andy rested his arm against Ladystar's side. The mare

nickered and then stomped her hoof impatiently, but Andy patted her flank. "Just give me a minute, girl."

He stepped away. His feet obviously had a mind of their own, because the last thing he should have been doing was exactly what he was doing, making a beeline straight to Aida, cutting her off before she reached her old compact car.

"Aida, please tell me where she is. I know she moved out of your place," Andy called. He strode toward Aida, really digging in to each step, swatting the papers in the air as if taking out a few flies here and there.

For a short woman in her seventies, Aida was quick as she darted around him. Andy spun around and jogged after her. This wasn't the average stroll he took when walking with a woman.

Aida yanked the hairnet off her short, graying bob, reaching behind her back to pull on her apron strings. "Andy Friessen, don't keep asking me, because I won't tell you." She jerked open the driver's door and tossed her apron and purse in. Andy gripped the top of the door so she couldn't slam it closed in his face again, as she'd done yesterday, last week, and every time he'd tried to talk to her after work. In the kitchen, she would ignore him and then order him out. When he didn't comply, she would threaten to quit.

Andy couldn't blame Laura for leaving him, really. After all, they never had a chance to get to know each other. There was no burning love between them, the kind where he would count the minutes—the seconds until he could see his wife again; the kind that would distract him and drive him crazy, his whole being sizzling in anticipation of that one touch, that smile, or just hearing her voice, the kind of deep love that would touch him inside his soul so that the thought of never seeing or hearing her again would shred his every last bit of good sense and he would question his will to live without her. No, there was none of that with Laura. He did, however, feel responsible for her even now, with these cursed papers burning a hole in his hand. Just what the hell was the matter with him?

Maybe it was because she was so young. She'd just turned twenty-one last week, and even though he hadn't seen her or heard from her, he had found himself buying her a gift—a solid gold locket. Of course, it remained wrapped upstairs in their room along with all of the other things he'd bought her. He had bought the gift on a whim, as he hadn't seen Laura or spoken to her since that day outside of the Seattle Hospital where Jed was recovering from surgery, when Andy had been a total ass. In hindsight, he'd love to go back and kick himself in the butt, to apologize, to not walk away and leave her standing there alone. She was honest, hardworking, and her only sin had been getting pregnant at fifteen with Gabriel and being cast into the street by her judgmental parents, who were too worried about how the situation would look and how it would influence Laura's younger brothers. Andy had never met her parents, and didn't plan on it, but he still couldn't soften his heart toward them.

He swung the paper in the air again. "She filed for divorce. I was just served. I need to talk to her, Aida."

The old woman stared straight ahead and said nothing.

"She asked for nothing, Aida. How is she paying rent? Where is she getting money from? Does she have a job? What about Gabriel?"

"Andy, let go of my door." Aida stared up at him with her plump, wrinkled face and her gray eyes, which were etched with tiny red lines as if they'd seen every good and bad thing in life.

Andy yanked out his wallet. "I need you to give her

some money. How is she going to look after herself?" He pulled out all of the bills, knowing there were only a thousand dollars there. He handed the stack to Aida, and she stared at the bills as if they were dirty. "Aida, did you give her the money I sent before? I know she didn't cash the check I gave you," Andy said, pleading.

She pursed her pale, wrinkled lips. She didn't look away, though she did appear to be considering what to say to Andy. Andy had no doubt she'd go to her grave without parting with one secret of where Laura was hiding.

"I gave her the cash, but do not ask again where the girl is, as I won't tell you. I promised her, Andy. She doesn't want to see you again," Aida said. However, bless her heart, she did fold the cash and tuck it into a side pocket of her purse before folding her plump body into the compact car.

"Aida, I want to see her and Gabriel. Could you ask her to meet me. Please?" Andy squatted down so that he didn't have to look down on the old cook.

"Andy, she has a right to be angry with you. You treated her horribly and made her feel as if she was a nuisance to have around. You may have married her to protect her and Gabriel, but the way you talked to her after you were married, it was as if she still worked for you. And she was a nice bed warmer, too, hey?"

Andy blushed, which was something he didn't do. Aida was right. He'd bedded her, but he hadn't shared one aspect of his life with her. Time did have a way of opening his eyes, especially when she'd taken nothing. He was worried about how she was managing to pay for anything just to survive, let alone feed her and Gabriel.

"Aida, I am a bastard, I admit, but I'm worried about her. Telling her I'm sorry doesn't even begin to make up for what I've done. I know words mean nothing, but please just ask her to meet me. How am I supposed to make things right if she won't see me?"

Aida gripped the steering wheel. She let out a heavy sigh. "Andy Friessen, I will talk to Laura, but I won't make you any promises."

Andy reached in and patted her arm because he sensed he was getting through to the tough old bird. If he could convince Aida he was sincere and win her over, she would be his best ally and his best hope to reach Laura. "I'll see you tomorrow, Aida, and thank you. Please tell her I'll go wherever she wants to meet, at any time, please..." Aida shut her door and Andy stood behind one of the ranch hand's pickups, watching as Aida drove away down the long, paved driveway, beside the manicured lawns and gardens, out to the highway.

His cell phone rang, and he yanked it from his back pocket. "Andy Friessen," he answered, distractedly watching the now empty driveway.

"Hey, Andy. This is Brian. I've got some news on that wife of yours," answered a familiar voice. Brian Rivers was a private detective that Andy had hired a few months back to keep an eye on Laura.

"If it has anything to do with her filing for divorce, I already know. I was just served by some law school dropout."

There was a clatter and brief silence on the other end. "No. I didn't know that. Well, how about that? So how much is she trying to bleed you for?"

"Not a damn thing, so I want to know where she's getting her money from. Is she still in that old house at the edge of town?" Andy watched Ladystar, who was tied to the rail outside the barn. The feisty thing was getting impatient, stomping her front hoof and pawing at the ground.

"Well, that's why I'm calling. She moved. Your cousin

and that pretty redheaded wife of his were there, and they picked her up. She doesn't have a car. She's staying out at their place. They built a studio above their barn and I'm pretty sure they moved her in."

Andy remembered Jed telling him just last week about the new studio. Hell, he'd even seen it; a cozy open loft with a kitchen, bathroom, living room, and bedroom all in one area. He thought Jed had told him it was for a manager he was hiring.

Then he wondered... No, it couldn't be. Laura was the manager and working for his cousin? Jed wouldn't do that to him and not say anything. But then, as the reality sank in and the stiff white paper burned a hole in his hand, Andy remembered that Diana, Jed's wife, had filed this petition, and not one of them had said squat. "I gotta go," he said.

"But, wait, don't you want to know—" Brian tried to interrupt.

"Not now, Brian. I've got to go. I have a cousin to visit."

CHAPTER

Two

"It's not much, but I think it's kind of fun and cute, and Jed and I will be right next door if you need us." Diana pressed her hand into the small of her back and rubbed her other hand with her gold wedding band over her almost eight months pregnant belly.

Laura's hair had started to grow out and was now shoulder length, and she kept it tied back in a high ponytail. "Diana, I don't know how to thank you and Jed for all you've done. This place is better than I could have hoped for. I love that clean smell of new wood." Laura took in the brand new loft, which had an antique double bed for her and a single bed for Gabriel, with lovely pink and green bedspreads. It was an open design, tastefully done, and even the appliances were brand new. She set her purse on the round kitchen table with four chairs. At the west side of the loft was a cozy living room with a green taupe sofa and chair and a plasma TV mounted to the wall.

Footsteps clattered up the stairs. Laura gazed over the wooden rail, watching as Jed followed Gabriel and redheaded Danny, who was just walking and insisted on mastering the stairs all by himself and yelling at the top of his lungs, "Mama, comin' up!"

"You've got your hands full with Danny there. Does he ever stop, Diana?" Laura smiled as she listened to the clomp and clatter of three boys: her five-year-old boy, Gabriel, who leaped up the steps; Danny, who crawled and patted each step; and Jed, who followed, encouraging his son.

"One more. Come on, you can do it." Jed was grinning from ear to ear, watching as Danny pushed himself to his feet and ran straight to his mommy.

"They're Friessen men; 'slow' and 'easy' aren't in their vocabulary," Diana muttered just as Jed stepped closer and lifted Danny, tossing him in the air while he giggled and wiggled. Then Jed leaned down and kissed Diana.

"That's not fair. I guarantee you I can take it slow and easy in some things you enjoy." He winked, and Diana gasped before clearing her throat.

"Laura, listen, I am grateful you've taken this job."

"Diana, Jed, I really do appreciate all this—and the job, even though I'm pretty sure you don't really need me."

"Oh, that's where you're wrong, Laura," said Jed as he put a kid-size cowboy hat on Gabriel's head.

"Cool hat. Ride horsey?" Gabriel beamed at Jed as he asked.

"Tell you what, bud. Let's let your mama get settled, and you come help me feed the horses," Jed answered. The sound of a vehicle coming down the driveway had him stepping toward the window.

"The fact is, Laura, we're the ones who are grateful," Diana said. "Jed wants to be on a horse, riding, teaching the kids, not cooped up in an office, doing paperwork. And I have my hands full with Danny and this one here." She rubbed the baby she carried in her large belly. "And I'm tired, too...."

"Well, I was wondering when he was going to show up," Jed interrupted. Danny just then decided he wanted down, so Jed slung him over his shoulder to distract him.

"Who's here, Jed?" Diana asked.

Laura felt a flutter of butterflies in her stomach when Jed glanced at Diana with a look that had her covering her mouth with her palm and turning away.

"My cousin, your husband," Jed said as he started toward the stairs. Gabriel was at the window with Jed, and he raced toward the stairs and started down.

"Gabriel, come back here!" Laura said, but this time he didn't listen, as he was out the door. She could hear him call out, "Andy, Andy."

Laura went to the window and gazed out at Andy, dressed as he always was in dark jeans and a long-sleeved dark shirt, but he wasn't as neat as usual. He lifted Gabriel in his strong arms and hugged him.

"You know, Andy has a lot of faults, but caring for Gabriel is not one of them." Diana was standing in the window, watching as her husband approached Andy. "I knew it was only a matter of time before he found out you were here. He was served this morning, too. He'll be furious, Laura. It was cold and impersonal."

"Diana, I don't want to see him again, ever. I just want him gone and out of our lives for good." Laura stepped back when Andy glanced up with those all-seeing hard blue eyes. At times, she'd swear they were etched in steel.

"Laura, how he treated you was horrible. We know that, and we all agree with you, but you can't keep avoiding him. He'll find out."

Diana turned solemn blue eyes on her. She'd been a true friend who was always there for her, even with her husband recovering from surgery. It had been a miracle when he came through okay, and Diana had even told Laura that life was too short for regrets.

"How does he know? You and Jed promised me you wouldn't tell him," Laura pleaded.

"Yes, we did, but don't forget that Andy's been having you followed," Diana said. "I have to tell you, Laura, my husband doesn't agree with your decision. He's honored it for now, hoping you'll come to your senses. Andy does have a right to know where you are. You should know he's offered to talk to Andy for you, too."

Laura felt a surge of anger shoot like a rocket through her as she processed what Diana had said. Her face felt warm, and beads of sweat popped out over her brow. She squeezed her fists. "He's been having me followed? Are you kidding me? What kind of sick—"

"Hello, Laura."

She didn't hear him come up, and what made it worse was that he was carrying Gabriel, who, by the looks of it, had no intention of allowing Andy to let him down. She could see how her son worshipped Andy, and that infuriated her. She was standing beside Diana, and it wasn't until Diana stepped back that Andy's eyes widened and his brows furrowed with something dark and furious.

"What the hell?" he said.

Laura pursed her lips and struggled with those damn emotions, second guessing everything she'd done, and placed her hand over her own large, swollen belly just as the baby kicked.

CHAPTER
Three

Laura could have heard a pin drop in that awkward second. Jed was now behind Andy, holding Danny, and for the first time today, Danny was quiet.

"Could you give us a minute?" Andy said, his icy gaze never leaving Laura. But she knew darn well he wasn't talking to her.

"Jed, I think maybe it might be better—"

"Diana, no. Come on. These two need to talk. It's past time. Andy, just a warning: Laura is living here, and there is some pretty heavy shit between you two. I can only imagine how mad you are, but be nice." Jed stepped around Andy until he glanced away from Laura. The look Andy gave him sent a chill through Laura that had her mind scrambling to find a way to leave. Andy could be a hard, unforgiving man—she'd sensed that in him. Laura dreaded what was to come next with him; it was sure to be nothing pleasant. She hated confrontations, and Andy was all about confronting everything, much like a bull in a china shop.

"Jed, can you take Gabriel down with you? And your

wife, too. Laura will be safe enough, for now." He directed a heated look at Laura, and she wanted to step back as she swallowed, but she couldn't, as she'd bumped the wall behind her.

"Andy, I'm sorry. I know you were served earlier today, but as Laura's lawyer..." Diana started toward Andy, but the look he gave her could have turned water to ice.

Jed reached out and took his wife's hand. "Andy, your wife will talk to you, but don't blame Diana. There's a lot to go around here in bad decisions, but you should know that Diana and I both insisted she tell you."

"Jed, right now I just want to talk to my wife alone." Andy kissed Gabriel on the cheek and put him down, but Gabriel latched on to his leg.

"No, Andy, up," he said.

"I'll see you after I talk to your mom. Go on with Jed."

Gabriel didn't look at Laura, and she was puzzled by the closeness he had now with Andy. When Gabriel had asked over and over where Andy was and when they could go home, she hadn't realized he was yearning for Andy's affection. After all, living in a big mansion had been comfortable, and she just thought he missed that.

Andy watched the stairs as Jed, Diana, Gabriel, and Danny descended in a noisy clatter, and his gaze landed on Laura the moment the door closed. He didn't take one step toward her. In fact, he appeared to pull away as he crossed his arms, which drew her attention to his wide, solid chest. The top two buttons were open, exposing the dark brown chest hair she loved to run her fingers through. He was a strong man, with solid pecs and six-pack abs, every part of him well muscled and lean. Unfortunately, Laura remembered all too well what it was like to be held in those arms, even if it had been for his enjoyment only.

Laura instinctively placed both hands over her round belly. "Hello, Andy."

"So what is this? You were planning on divorcing me, disappearing with my kid? It is mine, right?" he snapped.

Laura felt that slap, and her eyes burned as she blinked and looked away. "This is my child, Andy. You need not concern yourself or have any responsibility."

This was obviously the wrong answer. This time, he did step toward her, his hands fisted at his sides; she could feel his barely contained rage, pulsing around him like waves of a returning tide.

"I asked you if this is my child. Am I the father?" His voice was low and quiet as he asked her again, but this time his teeth were clenched when he spoke. He stopped right in front of her, so close that his breath was like a feather on her hair. She had to look up because he was so tall that the top of her head just reached his shoulders, and staring at his chest rattled her.

She briefly wondered if he was going to reach out and shake her. For a moment, she considered not telling him the truth. It would be easier, and he'd just go away, but she couldn't do that. "Yes, you're the father."

She was cowardly. When she looked away, she knew that, but she forced herself to look him in the eye. It was past time, but what she saw there took the wind out of her sails and made her doubt whether she had been the one who was wronged. He stared at her with tears in those icy blue eyes and inclined his head, staring at her as if he didn't know who the hell she was.

"Andy, I'm sorry. I didn't want to hurt you."

"Laura, how could you? Don't you know what a child of mine would mean to me? Did you know you were pregnant when you left?"

"Yes, I did." This wasn't going well. She suddenly felt like an evildoer.

"You had Diana file for divorce. Were you ever going to tell me I had a child, or did you plan to hide here at my cousin's and just hope that I never found out?" He was getting louder, and he was right in her face, so close that she could reach up and caress his cheek, run her hand over the dark whiskers of a day without shaving, that unclean look that made him look so...dangerous. She loved that look and wished he'd spent more time showing it. It made him touchable, human, and damn sexy.

"All I can say is that I'm sorry. But I didn't want you to be part of our life and treat me as if I was nothing but an irritation to you. I would never want my child to see that. My God, look at your parents!"

He leaned in, his nose almost touching hers, his eyes blazing with fire. "Don't you ever bring my parents into this and compare their actions to what you did," he said. She stepped to the side because she felt trapped. "You want a divorce—you can have it, but you're not keeping my child and living in some hovel. I can't stop you with Gabriel, but I can with this child."

This time, real fear hammered like bats beating their wings up her back. This was what she had feared would happen if he knew. "You're not taking my child from me. I'm his mother!" she shouted.

"Well, that's where you're wrong. You are not keeping me from my child. You've already had the courts take Gabriel away once, and it took me marrying you to get him back. You won't win this, Laura."

She didn't know where it came from, but she launched herself, fists flying, pounding his chest and screaming. "You're not taking my child from me!" She felt a twinge and then a sharper pain that had her stop and double over. "Argh!" she screamed out.

"Laura, what is it?" He had his arm around her shoulder, then sliding down her back, and she vaguely heard someone racing up the stairs in the background.

"What happened here?" Jed shouted.

Andy didn't wait as her abdomen tightened again, harder, and it hurt like hell. He scooped her up in his arms. "I'm taking her to the hospital. Get out of my way, Jed. She's my wife."

Andy carried her down the stairs, and Laura slid her arm around his shoulder after the tightening stopped. She let out a shaky breath.

Andy juggled her in his arms as he opened the door and slid her onto the passenger seat of his truck just as Gabriel came racing over.

"Andy, don't leave," he pleaded, throwing his arms around Andy's neck. When Andy bent down to a frantic Gabriel, Laura frowned, watching her son cling to the only man who'd ever shown him an ounce of caring.

"Hey, hey, bud, it's okay. Your mom just has to see a doctor. I'm coming back, I promise, okay?"

Diana appeared and leaned in the truck to Laura. "Are you okay? What happened?"

Laura shook her head as she rubbed her swollen belly. "I don't know. That scared me. It's too early for labor, Diana."

Diana reached in and took her hand. "Do you want me to come, too?"

Andy was right behind Diana, but he wasn't watching her with caring and concern, that love he'd always tried to hide. At one time, Laura had wished he'd look that way at her. No, he stepped back, holding the door open with that steely jaw set as waves of irritation rolled off of him and toward Diana. Yes, he was spitting mad, and it wasn't just at her. He was mad at Diana and Jed, too. What had she done?

"No. Could you watch Gabriel?" Laura asked.

"Yeah, of course." Diana stepped back and Andy moved in, and Laura didn't miss how careful he was not to touch Diana.

What he did do was fasten her seatbelt for her. His face was so close. He glanced at her and asked, "You okay?"

She flushed when his gaze took on a look of concern. For a moment, she wanted to believe it was for her. "I'm fine."

He stepped away and shut her door. She watched her tall, ruggedly handsome husband walk around the front of the truck, uttering something to Jed, then he slid under the wheel and started the engine. He was halfway down the driveway when he asked, "How far along are you?"

"Thirty weeks," she said as she stared straight ahead.

"So what is that in months?" he asked as the earlier venom in his voice changed to awkwardness. Or maybe it was just her.

"Seven months. Next week I'll be eight months."

"So how long did you know you were pregnant before you left?"

Her hand still lingered over her swollen belly as she remembered the positive result on the home pregnancy test the morning before Jed's surgery. "I'd just found out the day I left."

He slapped his hand against the steering wheel. "Dammit, Laura, why didn't you tell me?"

This time, she studied him as he glanced from the road to her. "Andy, the day I found out, I couldn't tell you. You treated me as if I was a nuisance. If I tried to talk to you, you brushed me off as if you had more important things,

Jed, Diana...oh, yes, Diana. You were more interested in spending time with her, being with her. I may be young, but I'm not a fool. I know you're in love with her." She didn't like the jealousy that always crept into her voice, because it was ugly, awful, and made her feel horrible.

"My cousin almost died. He barely made it through surgery, I had other things on my mind, so I'm sorry if I was distracted. I'm not proud of how I behaved."

"Would you have been happy for us if I'd told you then? Would you have decided to have a marriage with me? Would you have given us a chance for happiness?" She watched the range of emotions on his face as he glanced away then reached for his dark glasses and slid them on. "Oh, I see. Well, I guess there's my answer." She glanced out her side window, blinking back the sting in her eyes, refusing to cry one more tear over Andy as she'd done every night in bed alone since she left.

Four

Stretched out on her side in the emergency room of the local Lakewood Hospital, Laura waited for the doctor on call. Andy was standing just behind her, as she'd rolled to her side, giving him her back for two reasons, one being she'd long since lost the ability to breathe while lying on her back, and the other being that she couldn't face him any longer. The elastic in her maternity jeans was digging into her side. They were nothing fancy; she had picked them up at the second-hand store along with her orange flowered maternity shirt, but at least they were comfortable.

She yanked on the elastic a second time, and it snapped. "Oh, great." She held the dark elastic and then struggled to sit up.

"Laura, what's wrong?" He slid his hand over her shoulder, and she dropped back on her side.

"I'm uncomfortable. Can you find me a safety pin for this?" She lifted the wide elastic, which was worn on both sides. "I need to sit up."

Andy helped her up. She slid her legs over the side and

leaned back, pressing her hands into her lower back, which continued to ache as it had for the past few months. The curtain slid open, and a young, blond-haired doctor wearing a white overcoat and carrying a chart stepped in.

"Laura Parnell?" he said and glanced up at her. "I'm Doctor Avery. What seems to be the problem?"

"She doubled over in pain." It was Andy who spoke. "Her name is Laura Friessen, not Parnell. She's my wife."

"Oh, I see, but it says Parnell," the doctor said, glancing at Laura.

"We're separated. I never changed my name legally to Friessen anyway. It didn't seem right to keep using it," she spat out to Andy.

"Okay, Laura, it sounds like you're having some early contractions, because you're only thirty weeks. Are you still having them?" the young doctor asked.

"No. It only happened a couple times. I've been fine since I got here," Laura said, feeling foolish now for sitting here. "I'm probably wasting your time. I feel fine now."

The doctor studied Laura and then Andy. "You know, having a baby can be stressful, but if you're separated, I can only imagine the stress this is putting on you. Roll up your sleeve. I'm going to check your blood pressure." The young doctor wrapped the cuff around her forearm and listened with a stethoscope as he pumped it up.

"Hmm, okay. It's a little high." He ripped off the cuff.

"It says here that your doctor is a Doctor Hays. I don't recognize the name. Are you getting regular prenatal care?"

"She's a GP at the Hartford clinic. I see her regularly."

"That's the free clinic, isn't it?" the doctor asked.

She didn't need to look at Andy, because she could feel the man's irritation again and knew he'd have a few choice words for her. "Yes, it's the free clinic."

"Are you eating well, getting plenty of rest?"

"Yes to all of it," Laura snapped. She hated being judged, but she also noted the frown on the doctor's face, and she glanced at Andy.

"I'd like to get an ultrasound of the baby. Have you had one done yet?"

Laura shook her head. "There's been a waitlist."

When she glanced up at Andy, he roughly scrubbed his face with both hands and asked, "Who is the best OB around?"

Dr. Avery glanced up from Laura at Andy. "Well, that would be Doctor Richardson. She has a private practice in Arlington."

"I'll call her and schedule an appointment. You can take this other doctor off the chart, as I'll make sure Laura has the best."

Dr. Avery raised his eyebrows and smirked, scooting off the stool as if realizing he really didn't want to know much more about their situation. "Okay. I'll have the OB on call come down and do the ultrasound. Also, the nurse will be in to draw some blood. I've ordered a few routine tests, so relax for now." He slid the curtain open and left, sliding it closed behind him.

Andy studied Laura for just a second and then shook his head. He pushed the curtain open and called out, "Doctor Avery, could I speak with you a second?" Then he was gone, leaving Laura alone.

She plumped the pillow up and pressed it into her side. The curtain opened, and a woman wearing a lab coat and carrying a plastic bin filled with syringes and supplies strode in and set the bin on the side table.

"Laura Parnell?" she asked.

"No, it's Laura Friessen." Andy strode in again and put his hands on his very appealing hips. He stood in front of

Laura. The woman with short brown hair looked confused.

"Yes, that's me. Parnell is my maiden name," Laura finally said.

"Okay, well, I'm here to get some blood." The lab tech pulled out a piece of rubber tubing and tightened it around Laura's arm, taking four vials. "Okay, that's great. We're going to need a urine sample, too." She handed Laura a plastic cup. "Bathroom's just around the corner. You can leave it on the shelf when you're done," she said before leaving.

Laura set the plastic cup on the gurney and slid off to the floor. Andy's hand was instantly there, helping her. Her pants slipped, and Laura grabbed the top, pulled the broken elastic out, and sighed.

"I'll get a safety pin. Will they stay up in the meantime?" Andy asked.

"For now, I'll hold them up with my hand." Laura grabbed the cup and, holding her pants, waddled to the bathroom. Andy held the curtain open for her and followed on her heels.

Laura left the sample on the shelf in the bathroom. Her name, she noted, was scribbled on the side. Andy was waiting outside of the bathroom door and walked back with her to her little cubby and curtained-off area. He helped her back up on the gurney.

"Why don't you lie down?" Andy said.

"Could you raise the head of the bed up? I can't breathe when lying flat." Laura swung her legs up as Andy adjusted the bed until her head was high enough that she was almost sitting.

"I don't understand why you'd go to a free clinic and see some doctor who probably got his license from a Cracker Jack box." Andy leaned on the bed, watching

Laura with an odd look. She remembered all too well how he hid a part of himself well away from her, a part she couldn't access. She wondered if anyone could.

"I had no money, Andy. It's where poor people go," she said. Of course he'd have a hard time understanding; he'd never struggled a day in his life, a spoiled rich boy who could have anything he wanted at any time.

"I sent you money through Aida, even sent you a check that you never cashed. Why? Why wouldn't you have come to me for money? I don't understand, Laura." Andy crossed his arms and stepped back. She really couldn't believe how he didn't get it.

"That's your money, Andy, not mine. I'm no gold digger. I didn't feel entitled to it. You made me feel like a nobody, and I swore I would never rely on you again. Did you know that it took everything for me to hold my head up, bite my tongue when you treated me like a servant and an incapable twit? What would it make me if I took your money, Andy?"

He shook his head and ran his hand roughly up the back of his head, messing up his short, dark hair even more. "Well, not anymore. My child is going to have the best care. Now that I've found you, you're going to stop this nonsense and come home."

Laura felt a powerful fury sizzle to life inside her. She wanted nothing more than to pop Andy in the mouth with her fist. She was tired of his bullying. No, she was done and so past it that this was not going to happen. "Unless you plan on taking me by force and tying me up, which I believe is called kidnapping, you will not and cannot force me to go with you. You have tried to run my life, tried to tell me how to think, how to dress, where to go, what to do. I'm not a puppet, and—"

The curtain slid open, interrupting Laura.

"Hi, I'm Doctor Richardson," said the new arrival. "I just got an emergency page. I was in the hospital with one of my patients. Are you Laura Friessen?"

"Yes, she is." Andy spoke up before Laura could correct one more person.

"Doctor Richardson, where is Doctor Avery?" Laura asked.

The woman was stunning, with hair so dark it appeared mahogany. Her eyes were an unusual shade of blue that appeared almost green. "I was paged and asked to take over as your OB. Your husband here—"

"We're getting divorced, and I appreciate you coming down, but I have a doctor already, Doctor Hays," Laura snapped. She was so tired of Andy's high-handed behavior that any good sense she had had long since taken a hike. She wanted to yell and scream and get him to stop.

Another sharp pain ripped through her, and she curled on her side and yelled. She felt the doctor's hand on her arm, then her wrist, and heard someone calling out. A nurse appeared on the other side of her and fastened a blood pressure cuff to her arm.

"Let me know when it passes, Laura," the doctor said, still there beside her. "Let's get an ultrasound in here now, and let's monitor her for any further contractions." Dr. Richardson was giving orders.

Laura took a breath and wanted to close her eyes. She was so tired. "It's gone. Am I in labor? It's too early."

"Laura, I want to do an ultrasound and examine you. There seems to be a lot of stress here, and I think it would be best, Mister Friessen, if you'd step out for now. I'll come and speak with you after," Dr. Richardson said.

Andy rested his hand on Laura. When she glanced up, she expected to see defiance and maybe outright refusal, but what she saw was neither. She saw worry and something else that resembled caring. But it couldn't be. "I'll be right outside if you need me," he said.

Laura said nothing as he brushed the curtain aside and stepped out.

"Laura, you have every right to choose your own healthcare provider. No one, not even your husband, can choose that for you. If you'd like to continue using your current GP, you're entitled. What I'm concerned with is your blood pressure, which is high, and your stress level, which is the major contributing factor." The doctor accepted the chart from the nurse, who gracefully stepped out.

"I can't afford you," Laura said matter-of-factly.

"Ah, I see. Well then, let me ease your mind. Your medical costs are being covered by your husband," the doctor said. Laura started to set her straight again, but she gently touched her arm. "I mean your soon-to-be ex-husband. Just so you know, it doesn't matter who covers my costs; there is still patient-doctor confidentiality."

"So what you're saying is that you can't tell Andy anything unless I say it's okay?" Laura considered that and studied the striking woman who had such a warm demeanor.

"Yes."

"Okay. You can be my doctor."

"Great. Now that we have that out of the way, I'm going to get you to slide over on your back while I examine you. I know it's uncomfortable, so I'll try to be quick." The doctor lowered the bed and lifted Laura's shirt, pulling down the front of her pants and exposing her large belly. "You said you're thirty weeks?"

"Yes, why?"

The doctor shook her head and measured Laura's abdomen. "Oh yeah, you're way larger than you should be for thirty weeks. You could be further along. Let's get the ultrasound on you and take a look at this baby. That will give us a better idea of what's going on." She poked her head outside of the curtain and asked, "Is the ultrasound here?"

A nurse pushed the machine in as the doctor held the curtain open for her. "Your husband is getting mighty impatient out there. He asked if he can come in and see the ultrasound."

The doctor glanced at Laura. "It's your decision, Laura. If you don't want him in here, then we'll keep him out."

Laura's first response was to say no. Actually, hell no. But the fact that she'd hidden her pregnancy from Andy and had every intention of never telling him was starting to chip away at her conscience, and she couldn't get that picture of Gabriel clinging to him out of her mind.

"Go tell Mister Friessen that I'd prefer he not be here," the doctor said to the nurse.

"No, wait." Laura spoke up. "Let him come in."

"Are you sure?" Dr. Richardson asked in a way that made Laura truly believe she had her best interests at heart.

"Yes."

"Okay, but if you start to feel stressed or anxious, let me know, and I'll ask him to leave." The doctor slid the curtain open and popped her head out, and a few seconds later Andy strode in. He immediately went to Laura's side and stared at her exposed belly.

Laura couldn't help the flush that stole to her cheeks. She was flat out on a gurney like a beached whale and was feeling a gigantic pressure pushing into her.

"This may be a little cold." The doctor slid up a stool and squeezed a lump of jelly onto Laura's abdomen. Cold

was an understatement; the initial shock had her shudder-
ing. "Sorry. Are you ready to see this baby?"

"Yes, I am."

The doctor pressed the wand of the ultrasound onto
her belly and moved it.

"I can't see the screen," Laura said.

"I'm just going to have a look first and see... Oh my,
this is interesting."

"What is it?" Laura glanced at the doctor and then
over at a grinning Andy as he peeked around behind the
doctor at the screen.

"Is that...?" He pointed at the screen.

The doctor slid the screen over so Laura could see.
"Yes, Andy, that would be two babies."

Laura found herself settled in a private room in the hospital with a large window overlooking the parking lot. A strap was wrapped around the lower part of her abdomen, monitoring for any further signs of contractions—a stress test, as the doctor referred to it. She had been told to relax, which was without a doubt impossible, as Gabriel's face kept appearing in her mind. She was desperate to get back to him. Andy was lounging in the chair beside her, watching the monitor.

"Andy, can you call Jed and Diana and make sure that Gabriel is okay? I need to get out of here and back to him. He's going to start to worry." She pounded her fist on the edge of the bed.

Andy slid beside her on the bed. He was so strong that he could handle anything, and she found herself wanting to slip into that. But that would be a mistake. He frowned as if reading her mind.

"You're overthinking, Laura. Stop it and relax. I'll call and talk to Jed. Gabriel will be fine; I'll make sure of it. Laura, you have to relax. Remember what the doctor said:

When you get worked up, it will bring on early contractions."

"I know. I'm trying, Andy, just...you didn't make it easy," she shot back at him.

He looked up and took a deep breath. She could read him so well, but not this time. "I know, and I'm sorry, but you have to know that I wouldn't let anything happen to Gabriel, Laura."

"I know that," she said, and she did. That was one thing about Andy—he took care of things. "I just don't want him hurt, Andy. I didn't realize he cared for you so much, and I didn't think you cared for him."

He gave her a cutting glance. "Excuse me?"

"No, that's not what I meant. I knew you cared for him from everything you did, but I didn't believe you had feelings for him. I thought it was obligation. I didn't think..."

"Okay, look, let's just stop there." He cut her off sharply, letting her know he wasn't about to have this conversation. "Let me call Jed, and I'll be back."

This time, he touched her hand for what felt like an eternity. That touch was enough to set off all kinds of fireworks inside of her. Her body had obviously disconnected from her brain as she watched that sexy man, with the greatest ass she'd ever seen, walk out that door.

CHAPTER

Six

"Andy, I told you I don't want to go back to your mansion. I have my own place at Diana and Jed's. I'll be comfortable there," Laura said to him again.

Dr. Richardson had been perfectly clear to him when she pulled him aside after the stress test. She told him that Laura was refusing to stay and there was no reason to admit her. She instructed him to do whatever it took to keep her calm and not antagonize her. "Keep the peace, whatever it takes" was what she'd said. "Keep her happy, because thirty weeks is far too early for twins to be born." She would monitor Laura over the next week, but Laura was to take it easy and stay in bed for the next few days, rules that would be damn difficult to enforce as long as she wasn't living under Andy's roof. Short of tying her to the bed, what options did he have?

Yes, he was worried, damn worried. He still seesawed back and forth between being furious at having the carpet yanked out from under him and ashamed over how he'd treated her. She should have told him she was pregnant, and he didn't know how to get past the fact that she'd hidden something that he deserved to know. To him, that was the same as lying.

"Laura, you heard the doctor. You need bed rest, no getting up and chasing Gabriel around. You need to be waited on and looked after right now. It's too early for the babies to be born." A lump jammed his throat, because it had only just begun to sink in; the fact that he was going to be a father, and to twins, too. He glanced over, but what he saw had him swerving before he righted the wheel. Tears were sliding down her cheeks.

"Laura, what's wrong? Is it the babies?" He could take most things, but not her tears. Despite being a young woman and having gone through hell, she wasn't prone to tears or hysterics at the drop of a hat. He knew all too well that she hid her feelings. Hell, he was ashamed to admit that he liked the fact that she made herself blend in, never causing him any trouble at all. She shook her head, but when she finally turned to face him, what he saw was misery.

"What is it you're planning, Andy? I need to know. I can't live or wait holding my breath, wondering when you're going to yank the rug out from under me. You have money, power, and connections, and I know you're not above using them. You come from a family that abuses power. Hell, you could make sure I disappeared. I know that, with one phone call, you could take my babies away from me and never allow me to see them again. I'd fight you to the death. I want to know now, Andy."

"Laura, honey, stop. I'm not planning anything right now. I'm still dealing with the fact that you hid that you're pregnant with my babies, that you wanted to keep my babies from me and I never would have known. You wouldn't have told me, Laura, so let's just stop right now..."

"But you said you were going to take my babies away," she snapped, cutting him off.

He tightened his mouth and wanted to slam his fist against the wheel, but what the doctor had said was a better reminder than a smack upside the back of the head. He couldn't upset her, and it really stuck in his craw that she'd bring his stupid remark up now. He'd done a lot of idiotic things that he regretted later. Flying off the handle and snapping threats in anger were right up there with just about every dumbass thing he'd ever done.

He pulled over to the shoulder and parked, taking a minute to pull it together. He slid around and faced Laura, tossing his arm over her seat back. He was tempted to slide his hand over her shoulder, but the last thing he wanted was to upset her more, and his touch right now would most likely set her off. "Okay, let's just take a breath. I lost it. I'm sorry, Laura. I said what I did, and I could kick myself for reacting that way. I'm not a monster. I hope you know that."

She fidgeted with her fingers and locked them together. He wanted to run his hands over them to smooth away the tenseness, but he wondered again what she would do if he touched her now. He had no idea, so he didn't touch her.

"Laura?" he prompted her gently.

"No, I don't think you're a monster." She spoke so softly, and it stung because he recognized that beaten-down, withering voice from when she'd lost everything and had lived in her car. He never wanted her to suffer that horror again. "Are you going to try to take my babies away? I need to know, Andy." She sucked it up, looking at him with tears streaming down her cheeks, and not once did she try to hide her shame from him.

Boy, did he ever admire her courage. If he was the devil, she was facing him head on. "Laura, I won't do that, but I won't walk away, either. I want my children in my life, in my home, so we're going to have to work something out."

She frowned as she stared out the window. From her expression, he could tell she was thinking some pretty dark thoughts.

"Laura, I promise I'll be reasonable. Can you do the same?"

She didn't answer, but she did nod as she touched her mouth as if fighting back more tears.

Andy didn't linger anymore because he knew she was tired, which was probably making her unreasonable and stubborn, so he started the truck. A few minutes later, they pulled into Jed's, parking beside the barn.

"Well, thanks for the ride. I guess I'll be talking to you." Laura started to open her door, but Andy slid out and walked around, reaching her before she managed to step down. He shut the door behind her, and she glanced sharply at him.

"Well, let's get you to bed." Andy held out his hand, and she blinked. She opened her mouth to say something but shut it when Jed strode from the barn, with Gabriel racing toward Andy at the same time that Diana stepped from the house.

"What did the doctor say?" Diana shouted.

"Hey, you." Andy lifted Gabriel. "I told you I'd be back."

"Andy, stay," Gabriel said.

"You bet I'm staying, bud. Your mom's going to bed to get some sleep, and you and I are going to hang out."

"What do you mean you're staying?" Laura sputtered, and Diana appeared to stumble as she approached Jed.

Jed looped his arm around Diana's shoulder and

turned her the other way. "Andy, can I talk to you when you're done with Laura?"

Andy didn't put Gabriel down as he faced Jed. "When I'm done getting my wife to bed, I'll come and talk to you." He was irritated, and Jed must have understood, as he simply inclined his head and steered Diana back into the house.

"Laura" was all Andy said before she let out an annoyed huff of air and walked as gracefully as a woman pregnant with twins could walk around him and up the stairs to the loft.

"In bed, Laura," he said.

She sat on the edge of the lovely double bed. "Ouch." She leaned over and pulled at her waistband.

"What happened?" Andy put Gabriel down on the bed beside her.

"That safety pin jabbed me," she muttered.

"Well, take them off. I'll get your pajamas." He strode around the room. "Where are your pajamas, anyway?"

"Over there in that duffle bag. I haven't unpacked anything yet, as we just moved in." Laura pointed to a plain wooden kitchen chair, where a worn green duffle bag sat.

Andy didn't say a word as he rummaged in the bag and pulled out a worn cotton nightgown with blue flowers on it. He heard a squeak on the bed as Laura started toward him. "Sit down, Laura. I'll bring it over."

"I still need to get changed."

Andy handed her the nightgown, and she started toward the bathroom. "Laura, change right here, honey. Gabriel and I'll give you some privacy. Or do you need some help?"

She blushed and shook her head, and he smiled to himself, as he'd forgotten how shy she was. She'd never walked around naked. She always pulled on her housecoat after a shower or bath, and she always wore a nightgown to bed. Even though he removed it, she always pulled it on before getting out of bed.

Andy carried Gabriel down the stairs and out the open door into the barn. The horses were out in the pasture, and this was the first time in months that he had a chance to see all the updates that Neil, Jed's brother, had started in the barn and that Jed had finished. Six stalls for six horses, with the fresh smell of wood, manure, and hay. He loved the smell, always had. But you had to love horses and this way of life, as he'd heard from city people who wrinkled their noses and nearly gagged from the pungent odor.

"What do you think, bud? Is your mama changed by now?" Andy put Gabriel down and held his hand.

"Yes," he said as he beamed up at Andy.

"You're talking much better," Andy said. He was, since he hadn't said a word until Andy married Laura and found him the right help. He held the little boy's hand and started up the stairs. "Laura, we're coming back up. Are you changed?"

The bed squeaked. "Yes."

Gabriel clomped noisily up the wooden steps, and it echoed. Andy realized Laura wouldn't get much rest, listening to that. Gabriel raced straight to Laura, who was perched on the bed in the thin nightgown, one he'd never seen before. It looked worn and old, much like the clothes she had on earlier.

"Mama, hungry." Gabriel started to climb on the bed.

"Whoa, bud, just a second. Hop down. Let your mom get some rest." Andy lifted Gabriel off the bed at the same time that Laura slid off. "Laura, stay in bed." Andy put Gabriel on the floor beside the bed.

"He's hungry. I need to feed him. It's getting late, and I'm hungry, too."

Andy put his hands on her shoulders this time. "No. Back to bed. I'll feed Gabriel and you, too." He glanced over at the tiny kitchen that held a new fridge, a stove, a kitchen sink, and one long countertop. It was very nice, doable. When he faced Laura, she was frowning at him with an odd look.

"Andy, do you even know how to cook?" she asked.

The fact of the matter was that he'd never been allowed in the kitchen at the Friessen mansion to cook. Yes, he'd gone in and made a sandwich, heated soup, but anyone could do that.

"Of course. I can do enough to get by. I make a mean grilled cheese."

"Andy, I don't know what there is for food. I didn't have a chance to buy anything yet. But I think Diana put some things in the fridge to get us started."

Andy yanked open the fridge and found it well stocked. He pulled bread, butter, and cheese from the fridge. There was sliced chicken and tomatoes, as well, and he pulled a couple of apples from the bottom drawer of the fridge.

"Where are the fry pans, cutting board?" Andy asked as he opened cupboard doors and the row of drawers and heard the bed squeak again. "Laura, stay in bed. I'll find it."

"It would be easier to just let me do it," she snapped and then rubbed her bare arms.

"Are you cold?" Andy asked.

"Yeah. I have a sweater in the bag over there, as well."

"I'll get it." He rummaged the bag and found a light brown sweater that had a button missing on front and fuzz balls all over it. "Where did you get these clothes?" He strode to the bed and held the sweater up when Laura scooted forward.

"The second-hand store," she stated quite sharply. "It was all I could afford, Andy, and it's not as if I'll be wearing them much longer."

"Laura, I'm not putting you down, so don't take it that way, but I sent you money through Aida, and I wish you would have come to me." He shook his head because he wished he could go back all those months and do a lot of things over.

"Andy..." Laura yanked the elastic from her hair, and the ends brushed her shoulders. She tucked it back behind her ears and then glanced up at him. He would swear that her green eyes were tinged with gold in this light, and this time she couldn't hide her weariness.

"Look, let me feed Gabriel, and I'll get you something to eat, too. Are you okay with a chicken sandwich? It looks like Diana stocked things pretty well."

This time, she smiled, not brightly, but a hint of one that touched the corners of her lips, one that actually removed the nervous shadow from her eyes. "That would be fine. Thank you."

Andy hesitated and then pulled a blanket at the foot of the bed over her. He reached for the second pillow and fluffed it behind her. "Comfortable?"

Her face tinged a hint of pink again, but this time she wouldn't look his way. "Yes. Thank you."

A thump had Andy turning back to the kitchen. Gabriel picked up one of the apples from the floor and started to take a bite. Andy hustled. "No, bud. Let's wash it first."

Gabriel beamed at Andy, his baby white teeth and bright eyes filled with love for him.

"How about you help me make a sandwich for your mom, too?"

"Yeah, Mom. Me and Andy will cook!" Gabriel shouted.

And Laura laughed.

How could she come to terms with a man she thought she knew as a selfish, arrogant, controlling jerk, but who spent the evening playing with her son, waiting on her, watching over her, and noticing every time she was upset, uncomfortable, or just plain bored. It wasn't the fact that he was making sure the babies, his babies, were nurtured and kept safe in her unstable womb. He seemed to genuinely care about her, about Gabriel, with each touch and caress and every time he moved the pillow, pulled the blanket around her, brought her water or food, and helped her from bed to go to the bathroom. Laura couldn't for the life of her begin to make sense of it, because she'd already decided to leave him, divorce him, and never have anything more to do with him. Now she felt absolutely wicked for even thinking of hiding his children from him.

She'd watched in awe as he patiently showed Gabriel how to butter bread. When he started to show him how to cut the cheese with a knife, Laura had jumped, and he must have seen her, but he leaned over Gabriel, who stood beside the table, holding the knife as Andy's large hand guided him, and said, "Laura, everything's under control." She'd leaned back, feeling as if she'd gone through the washer on the ringer cycle. She'd never seen this side of Andy before, and the fact was that he made a decent sandwich—chicken, tomato, lettuce, and cheese, and she'd enjoyed every bite. He'd even washed the dishes, and Gabriel helped, giggling and beaming up at Andy. This was worse than a nightmare because she couldn't walk away from this. Gabriel would never forgive her now.

At this moment, she was almost in tears, because here he was, reading Gabriel a story, after he'd bathed him in the small corner bathroom and dressed him in the blue Cookie Monster pajamas she'd also picked up at the second-hand store.

Andy kissed Gabriel on the forehead and tucked him into the single bed against the opposite wall. "Say goodnight to your mom, bud."

"Night, Mom." Gabriel grinned from ear to ear as he gazed over at Laura.

Just watching the scene had something disturbing squeezing deep inside her. It wasn't sudden; it had crept up throughout the day and through each second that Andy had spent with Gabriel tonight. He could be the perfect father, the perfect man and role model for her son. She cleared her throat but nearly choked when she whispered, "Goodnight, Gabriel. Have a good sleep."

This was all so confusing. What did Andy want? Why hadn't he left, and why was he taking such an interest in Gabriel? Her throat felt all scratchy and tight, but that was only because she wanted to tuck her face in the pillow and cry those thousand tears she'd cried almost every night for Andy. All she'd ever wanted was to be loved.

What he'd done today was horrible, cruel, and she

wanted to scream and yell "Why?" He had stayed, caring for her tonight and today at the hospital in a way that made her feel important, special, but she also knew she wasn't any of that to him, not in the way she wanted to be. It was the babies. She was just the vessel, a warm cocoon for a rich man's babies, and that was something she could not allow herself to forget. He was powerful, he was rich, and his family was dangerous.

"Are you all right?" He brushed his finger across her brows.

"Yeah, fine," she blurted as she pulled back, her skin burning from the spark of his touch.

"You look worried about something, upset." He was watching her, studying her as if he knew what she was thinking, and she couldn't have that.

"No, I'm just..." She couldn't think of what to say when her brain suddenly blanked out. That always happened when Andy stood so close to her and watched her with compelling blue eyes that could set her soul on fire, so she shut her mouth and shook her head.

He sat right beside her on the bed so his hip pressed into hers. She knew all too well what those slim hips and tight abs looked like naked and pressed against her hips, nestled between her thighs. It was almost too much heat for her, so she squirmed and tried to slide over and away from him.

"You all right? You look uncomfortable."

He wouldn't even look away. Uncomfortable—hell yeah. And it was all his fault. "Just stiff is all."

"Can I?" He rested his hand over her swollen belly, where the babies had been kicking furiously for the last hour.

He was connecting with her babies. She wanted to scream and yell at him, "Hell no! Keep your hands off!"

but her body was betraying her. The reality was that she wanted him to touch her, to run his hands over every square inch of her.

He didn't wait for her to say anything, but then, she couldn't get her tongue to move. The damn thing had thickened, and her throat had completely dried up as he invaded her space. My God, he even smelled good, and his scruffy jaw...she longed to reach up and run her hands over it.

His touch sent shockwaves through her, and the babies responded in kind. She'd swear they'd jumped from his touch, as if they knew that Andy was their daddy. He smiled that charming, boyish grin she'd only seen a few times. Never once had he smiled just for her.

"Wow, that's amazing. Did you feel that?"

For a moment, she felt herself being pulled into his joy, just like a little boy's first Christmas; but she had to look away, to move away from his touch, because she'd never again be treated as if she was nothing. Andy Friessen could turn on a dime, and she'd never play second again. "Yeah, I did. Listen, I'm tired." She scooted over and lifted his hand off of her belly. She couldn't look at him even though she could feel the sharp change in him as if she'd just ripped away all his joy. So why was she feeling guilty? She wasn't the bad guy here.

Andy stood up and stepped back. "I'm going to have a word with Jed. I'll be right back." He said it sharply, and it took her a minute to realize his meaning.

"Aren't you going home?"

He gave her a questioning glance that she couldn't read. He shook his head. "No, I'm not going anywhere." Then he turned and left down the stairs, and she could do nothing but listen like a stunned woman as the door at the bottom of the stairs opened and shut behind him.

How the hell was she supposed to relax if he wasn't going to leave? She bolted straight up, which was a mistake, as she felt a sharp jab in her ribs. As gracefully as she could, she stepped out of bed and over to the window above the kitchen sink, which overlooked Diana and Jed's house. She watched as her long-legged husband, all lean and sexy, strode over and up to the wraparound front porch Jed had recently built. It was one of many upgrades, including the extension that had added three more rooms and a family room to the back of the house. Jed stepped out, and a minute later Diana did, too.

Jed didn't allow his wife to linger beside him. He always swept her close to him, his arm around her shoulder, hugging her to him. That was what Laura envied about Jed and Diana, their love. Just being around them, she was pulled into that radiance. She wanted that, but Andy had never once treated her that way, because he loved Diana. She wondered if Jed knew where his cousin's thoughts went. Laura was pretty sure Diana didn't have a clue, but she'd never asked. Andy's concern for Diana had always been over the top. In the beginning, she'd chalked it up to the fact that she was family, but, come to think of it, that was just plain stupid. Andy wasn't just overly concerned about his cousin's wife—it was obvious he had the hots for her.

It took a second for Laura to realize that all three of them were staring at her from where they stood. Andy looked none too happy, and his normally neat dark hair was sticking up here and there as if some woman had just run her fingers through it. The thought made her blood boil, but she was embarrassed for staring out at them, so she stepped back away from the window, feeling as if she'd just been caught doing something she shouldn't. Well, actually, spying on Andy, Diana, and Jed was a pretty low thing to do.

Laura glanced at a now sleeping Gabriel, tucked into his cozy single bed with the comforter pulled up under his chin, and had taken one step back to bed when the door opened and footsteps pounded up the stairs.

"What are you doing out of bed?" Andy snapped in a low, sharp tone as he glanced at Gabriel, who was still soundly sleeping.

Laura couldn't think of what to say, because blurting out that she was standing there ogling him was the last thing she wanted to admit. Instead, she crossed her arms, tucking her fingers into the warm brown sweater, and said, "You're still in love with Diana, aren't you?"

There, she had said it, but she felt like an absolute idiot as he said nothing, glancing away as if he couldn't figure out what language she was speaking.

"No, I'm not in love with my cousin's wife."

She wanted to yell and scream and hit him, but instead

she clenched her fists tighter in her sweater and stepped around him "Bullshit," she whispered as she stepped back to the bed, but Andy, being Andy and never walking away from a fight, was right behind her. Hell, he was right in her space again, her tall, muscular, very male husband. Inside him lurked a strong alpha and dangerous predator that he controlled on a very loose leash. She could feel it sizzle now, just below the surface, and she knew she was provoking it in him much like a fool would poke at a poisonous snake. She kept her back to him and pulled back the covers of the bed, doing her damnedest to remain calm, but inside she was shaking so hard she wondered if he could feel it.

He didn't just touch her; he slid his arms around her, one just under her breasts and the other over her hips, just under the swell of her belly. He pulled her against him, and she could feel the hard ridge of him pressed into her. She froze as he slid his lips against her and whispered, "Does this feel like I'm in love with Diana?" He brushed his lips over her ear and into her hair.

Like an inexperienced fool, she gasped and leaned into him, and he didn't stop as his hand pressed lower into her curls and over her sex. He held her like a prisoner against him. She couldn't have stepped away if she wanted to, as her legs would have given out. His warm breath was a whisper on her neck, which she couldn't help but offer to him. Then he stopped in an instant, his arm loosening under her breasts from where he had held her up. The hand that had touched her so intimately fisted at his side as he stepped back, but when her knees buckled, he scooped her up as if she didn't weigh more than a feather and set her on the bed with ease.

"I'm sorry," he said. He didn't try to touch her now, stepping back and pressing his fingers into the space between his brows, shutting his eyes for a second. Good. Maybe he was as rattled as she was.

"I'm tired. I'd like to go to sleep."

"Fine. I'll get in the shower." His tone had a rough bite to it.

"You can't stay here, Andy. You have a home, a big one, to go to." She was feeling desperately overwhelmed because she feared a long, sleepless night, and the last thing she wanted was all that male hardness pressed up against her in this small, cozy, double bed, not because she feared him or didn't want him, but because she was freaking out inside. She wanted to toss all of her self-respect out the window and say to hell with fighting him, hiding from him, and running away from him. She wanted to sleep with him, to touch him, to be with him, but when she looked up at him, he wasn't smiling. His handsome face seemed to be made of granite, immovable, and then he leaned forward, putting his face just inches from hers so that she shared his breath.

"No," he growled, and then he was gone into the bathroom.

She listened as the shower came on, and she sagged as if releasing her breath. "Oh my, now what?"

The cold hard fact was that she was about to get her wish, the one thing she shouldn't have wanted.

To say it had been a frustrating night for Andy, as he lay pressed against Laura's sweet, tight ass, going through pure and absolute torture, was like saying Mount Everest was a little big. He had never experienced that kind of agony, ever, and it had turned a mild case of insomnia into a long, painful, and sleepless night.

After all, he wasn't a monk. He never had been. Even before he'd married Laura, he'd had a healthy sexual appetite, and he sated it often. Having Laura, who was young and gorgeous, with a slim waist, tight ass, and full, high breasts that he'd sampled often, had been a welcome and appreciated perk. He could have kicked his ass now for not treasuring her. The fact was that he cared for Laura. He just hadn't realized how much until she was gone. The last six months, he'd seen no relief. Andy had always had women falling at his feet, racing across the street just to get his attention, tossing him their phone numbers, and he knew he could have snapped his fingers and had a woman on her back in two seconds, ready and eager to satisfy his insatiable needs, but he just couldn't do it.

As he watched the sun come up, feeling as if sand had scraped the back of his eyelids, Laura rustled beside him and snuggled in closer, her head resting on his shoulder, her hand pressed into the soft, dark hair of his chest. His babies poked into his side. She slid her leg over his, and he thought he'd go blind in agony as he groaned with need. It took him a minute to realize she was awake. She stiffened, and her hand moved lower, over his tight washboard abs and lower still, as if she was trying to seduce him.

Andy kissed the top of her head and grabbed her hand. "Laura, stop." He pulled away, attempting to slide out of bed, and didn't miss the tears that glistened in her eyes. "What the...?"

Her cheeks glowed a light shade of pink. Hell, he was embarrassed. With his maleness prodding into her, she had to be humiliated, but he couldn't take how she seemed to pull into herself as she tried to scoot upward, casting her gaze at the bed and away from him.

"Laura, don't do that."

"Do what? I don't know what I was thinking. There must be something wrong with me. I thought you wanted me." She refused to look at him when she spoke, and this time she did slide off the bed onto the cold floor.

What did Andy do? Well, he reacted as a man exhausted and emotionally pushed to the brink. Gone was any attempt that mildly resembled diplomacy as he ripped back the sheet and stalked naked, fully aroused, around the bed. Laura gasped, and her face burned brighter. She should have been terrified, and maybe she was, as her eyes flared with something that resembled shock. He backed her up to the bed until the back of her legs bounced off the mattress and she fell back as he loomed over her, one arm on either side of her.

"The only thing I want to do is throw you back on this

bed and bury myself inside your softness, to ride you like an animal to give myself some relief. But I won't. I can't do that to you, because the last thing I want to do is hurt you. If you think for one minute I don't want you..." He growled and grabbed her hand, wrapping it around his hard length, which nearly blinded him and brought him to his knees, further proving that his brain had obviously taken leave. "That's all for you, baby," he snapped.

"Andy?" Gabriel rustled in the other bed behind him.

Andy yanked the quilt off the bed and wrapped it around his waist, and Laura gaped, her face pink. She scurried off the bed and into the bathroom, shutting the door with a sharp thud.

Gabriel rubbed his eyes. "I'm hungry."

"I bet you are. Let me just..." Andy flexed his fingers through his short hair, spiking it more, and snatched the clothes he'd tossed over the kitchen chair.

When Laura came out of the bathroom, she glanced shyly at Andy, still wearing that long worn nightgown. In the morning sun that streamed through the window, he could see the outline of her slender legs. Her nipples and full breasts were pressing against the tight bodice.

"Let me grab a quick shower"—*a cold one*—"and then I'll get you and your mom some breakfast."

"Andy, I can make breakfast. I'm pretty sure there's cereal and milk. I can do that much." She was fidgeting, rubbing her bare arms, glancing over his shoulder in a very obvious way, too embarrassed to make eye contact.

"No. Back to bed, and then we're going home."

Gabriel squealed and leaped from bed. *"Yeah!"* he cried, and he started jumping up and down in front of Andy. "Home with Andy!"

Laura crossed her arms. In a flash, absolute fury fell over her. "Andy, I already told you—" she snapped just before a sharp tap on the door at the bottom of the stairs interrupted them.

"Come in," Andy shouted, and the door opened. Andy glanced over the railing, and Gabriel raced to the stairs and started down.

"I just wanted to come over and see how you are this morning, if you guys need anything." Diana came up the stairs. Jed was right behind her, carrying Danny. "Good morning, Gabriel."

"We're going home. Andy's taking us home," Gabriel chirped excitedly to Diana.

Diana's face flushed when she glanced at Andy with the quilt wrapped around his waist, standing bare chested, holding his clothes.

"That's great news," Jed said as he stepped around Diana, still carrying Danny, and swung Gabriel up in his other arm.

"Andy, I have a job here," Laura started to say, until Jed and Diana exchanged a concerned look.

"Laura, you can't work. You already know that. The doctor already told you that you're on bed rest until further notice. You can't push it after what happened yesterday."

"Laura, the job's here for you, but you need to listen to your doctor." Diana was pressing her fingers into the small of her back as she stepped closer to her. "I want to talk to you for a minute." She swept her hand toward the bed. "Sit down, Laura. Andy, could you give us a minute?"

Andy stared at Diana. She was beautiful—and very pregnant with his cousin's child. They had a past so filled with pain and hurt, all that emotional crap, all because of him. He wondered as he watched her whether what he felt was guilt over his part in turning her world upside down as a teen.

"I'm going to grab a shower and get dressed." He

didn't address Diana, speaking instead to his wife, whose head snapped up as if she couldn't believe he was talking to her. He closed the bathroom door behind him, listening to the murmur of voices, and cranked on another chilly shower.

CHAPTER
Ten

"Why don't you come down with me, and you can help feed the horses? Come on, go grab your shoes." Jed set Gabriel down, and he scurried to where the small cowboy boots Jed had given him were tossed on the floor beside his bed. "You okay with that, Laura?" Jed asked.

All Laura could do was nod like a stumbling fool. Then she realized Gabriel wasn't even dressed. "Jed, maybe I should get some clothes on him." She started to get up, but Diana grabbed her arm and patted it.

"Sit down, honey. The horses really don't care what he's wearing." Diana inclined her head to Jed, and he took Gabriel and Danny down the stairs.

"You okay?" Diana asked.

Laura glanced at the closed bathroom door and listened to the water running. "I don't know what to make of him."

Diana too glanced at the door and back at her with deep blue eyes that didn't seem too concerned. "Andy has always been a hard man to read. But, Laura, you can't keep his child from him, and I told you that before, when we filed for divorce."

"You said you agreed with me," Laura snapped.

"Oh, wait a minute. That's not exactly what I said, Laura. I said I agreed with your reason to leave, not about the baby. He didn't treat you very well, I agree, but hiding his child from him goes against everything. You need to be honest with him, too."

"Yeah, but he doesn't even love me. I can't go back to that. It just about killed me, being dismissed and treated as if I worked for him. Yesterday, he threatened to take my babies away."

Diana reached for her hand. "Laura, I think he cares for you more than you think, and I won't let him take your babies away. But I have to say this—what I saw yesterday was how much Gabriel adores him. You need to talk to Andy, spend some time with him, because no man would do what he did for you yesterday if he didn't care."

"He cares about the babies, Diana, but he's in love with you. So how do you think that makes me feel?"

Diana's eyes widened, and she gasped as she gave a sharp glance at the bathroom door, obviously worried Andy would hear them. "You're wrong, Laura. He doesn't love me." Her expression was suddenly filled with deep hurt. "We share a horrible past. Whatever his feelings are, it's not love."

"Diana, I've seen the way he looks at you when Jed..." She pressed her lips tight as if realizing she was about to say too much.

"When Jed had his accident, Andy was there for me. It was a bad time, Laura. Andy's had feelings for me, and he may be confused by them. I was so deeply in love with him as a kid that I worshipped him, but we are dynamite together, in a bad way. There was a powerful hate between us, too, and I don't really want to get into it. But it's not love he feels for me, Laura. He couldn't ever love me. He may have thought he wanted me, but, Laura, you need to understand, sometimes we really want something for all the wrong reasons. We pray for it and think we'll die without it, but those unanswered prayers are the blessing. It's when you get it that you realize it wasn't what you wanted and is the worst thing for you. That's me with Andy."

"She's right."

Diana gasped, and Laura stared at Andy's deep blue eyes, flecked with gray and something different that she hadn't seen before.

"I didn't hear the shower turn off," she said.

He shut the door. His damp hair was sticking up all over as if he'd just rubbed a towel through it and walked away.

"I'm going. Andy, you and Laura have a lot to work out." Diana groaned as she stood up. "You're going with Andy, right?" Diana waited for her to respond.

Laura panicked for a minute because, to her, it really seemed as if Diana had just thrown her to the wolves, or namely one wolf, a definite predator who she was terrified of—not from fear but from her reaction to him. He always had this hold on her, a powerful, deep wanting of him. Now, as she sat there, rumpled and frustrated, she let out a heavy sigh. She worried deep down that she was about to jump head first off a cliff, and she hoped it wasn't a decision she'd regret. "Yes," she replied.

S he really didn't have much to load up. Andy had never unpacked their bag of clothes the night before, and she wondered now if it was because he had planned all along to take her back to his place—the Friessen mansion, a beautiful estate that wasn't in the least bit comfortable. A comfortable home was one she could relax in, with a few bedrooms, a cozy living room, and kitchen. Not a ten-thousand-square-foot mansion that was more like a palace filled with priceless artwork, and trinkets that she always worried Gabriel would touch or break, things that were absolutely useless except to show everyone how much money the Friessens had to throw away. Andy never worried about "the stuff," as he called it. He didn't have much use for it. After all, it belonged to Caroline, his mother.

Caroline was the most uptight, snobbish, cruel woman Laura had ever met. The only thing Laura had been thankful for was that she'd left the estate shortly after Andy married her. Laura had overheard Jules saying that Caroline had gone back to their other house in the south of

France. Apparently, she preferred it there anyways, and that was just peachy with Laura because she didn't know how she could face Andy's parents after they'd treated her as if she was something dirty and smelly that they'd scraped off the bottom of their shoes when she'd worked there as a maid. Even after she'd married Andy, they treated her as if she was a nobody.

"Hey, bud, after I get your mom settled in bed, how about I take you riding?"

Laura had been gazing out the side window of his fancy truck. When she glanced over, Andy was grinning in the rear-view mirror at Gabriel.

"Yeah...I want to ride horsey," Gabriel squealed excitedly. Andy laughed.

Laura knew she should be happy to see Gabriel so happy, but she worried this was just a passing phase for Andy. Her deep-rooted fear of being tossed out and rejected was still there. She didn't have a clue what Andy really wanted. He said he wouldn't take the babies from her, even though he'd threatened in anger that he would. If a man threatened something, would he not follow through? She was about as experienced with men as a nun, but then, a nun wouldn't have a child out of wedlock at the ripe young age of sixteen.

"What's wrong, Laura?"

She shook her head. She couldn't tell him and certainly couldn't talk in front of Gabriel.

"You were frowning," Andy said.

"Was I? I didn't realize. I was just thinking, is all." She took a look at her son, who was in his car seat, fastened in the backseat behind Andy. He was beaming ear to ear. She faced forward just as Andy turned down the long, paved driveway that led to his estate, or rather, his parents' estate.

Laura gripped the dashboard and felt her stomach

tighten and pitch when she spied a black limousine parked out front with the servants unloading luggage. Caroline stood in the open back door, the limousine driver holding it open for her.

Andy braked hard behind the limo. "Stay here" was all he said to her as he hopped out. Caroline slid off her dark glasses. She was dressed in a cream-colored suit, with dark red nails and perfect makeup. Even her shoulder-length, light hair appeared as if she'd just come from a salon. But then, Caroline was from old money, so she may very well have had a stylist on her payroll to appear when summoned.

Caroline reached her hand, with long, manicured nails, up to Andy's whiskered cheek and then yanked it away as if disgusted by the way he looked. To Laura, he looked unbelievably sexy, his short hair sticking up in spikes here and there as if she'd run her fingers through it. His third day of not shaving, wow! Andy was now walking straight for her with a scowl on his face. His mood could change with a snap of his fingers, she'd noticed, especially when his mother was around. He pulled open her door, but she made no move to get out.

"Maybe I should go back to Diana and Jed's."

Andy said not a word as he reached around her and unfastened her seatbelt, then pressed his hands to her cheeks. "No," he said, then reached in and lifted her out. She felt poleaxed when his hands left her, and she wanted to reach back and grab him when Caroline's eyes fixated on her swollen belly and her mouth opened and shut before she could say a word. Laura knew enough of Caroline's moods to recognize that she was shocked by Laura's condition. Maybe she'd have a few choice things to say to her, as well. Laura was pounded by wave after wave of inadequacy. She dropped her gaze and flushed when she realized Caroline may have been more appalled by the drab, second-hand, and very baggy overalls she wore over a faded blue cotton shirt. They were a size too big, but comfort and fitting were all she cared about at this point. She certainly couldn't afford to go to one of those fancy schmancy maternity stores where a simple t-shirt could cost a small fortune.

"Let's go." Andy carried a very quiet Gabriel and looped his other arm around Laura, urging her forward.

"Well, this is quite a surprise. Pregnant! I guess you'll never be rid of her now, Andy." Caroline's voice was laced with enough venom that Laura felt the sting as if she'd just been bitten. Laura didn't realize she had stopped and was gawking like a fool.

"Mother, I will remind you that Laura is my wife, and she is carrying my babies. Don't disrespect her." Andy's arm tightened around Laura as he urged her up the stairs to where several of the house staff lingered at the front door, juggling all of Caroline's bags.

The distinct clickety-click of Caroline's heels followed directly behind them. Laura could even feel Caroline's hatred burning into her from behind.

"Jules!" Andy shouted as he helped Laura up the stairs with Gabriel still in his arms.

Laura didn't miss the wide eyes on Gabriel as he stared back over Andy's shoulder at Caroline in fear, his tiny little hands holding on to Andy for dear life.

"Oh, sir..." Jules hurried from the kitchen, and her eyes widened in shock as she stared at Laura. She then firmed her lips and jumped when Caroline Friessen stopped in the middle of the palatial entryway as if she was the queen showing up for the ball. Everyone seemed to stare as they climbed up the stairs.

"Jules, I need you up here now," Andy barked. He didn't even try to hide his irritation.

"Yes, sir."

They climbed the stairs, and someone else followed. Laura didn't turn to see because Andy wouldn't let her go until they reached their bedroom door, the same bedroom she'd shared with Andy every night while she'd lived under this roof and slept with him in his bed.

The room hadn't changed. The four-poster mahogany bed still filled the center of the richly decorated room, painted with the same expensive colors, gold and white. The fireplace with the white mantel, the plush chairs positioned in front just so, and the furnishings—everything was exactly the same.

She felt so much the country bumpkin, out of place, and wished that she was back at Diana and Jed's in the loft above the barn.

"Jules, Laura is on bed rest until the doctor says otherwise. I'll need you to help out." Andy's hand was in the small of her back, guiding her to the bed, where he set Gabriel down, too. "Let's just get your mom settled, and then I'll take you out."

Laura perched on the edge of the bed and felt all the color drain from her face when Caroline stepped into their bedroom, crossed her arms in a stance that let Laura know she was darn well pissed.

"Anderson, I would like a word with you, now," she ordered. She didn't ask, and every part of Andy hardened a little more. Laura wanted to weep. She didn't want the attentive man who'd been with her at the loft to go away.

"Sir, I can help Laura get settled." Jules stepped closer, and Laura rested her hands on the bed behind her and scooted back a little further.

Gabriel grabbed hold of Andy's arm and started

whimpering; Caroline was making him nervous. Hell, Laura had to fight the urge to grab Andy's other arm and hide behind him. "Andy..." Her voice trembled.

She wondered for a moment if he knew, because he reached up and touched her cheek with his large, rough hand. It was pure instinct that had her slapping her other hand over his, holding tightly as if he were her lifeline.

"Laura, it's going to be okay. Jules, can you take Gabriel down to the kitchen? I'm going to get Laura settled. Mother, I'll speak with you when I'm done." He didn't look at Jules or Caroline when he spoke. He held Laura's gaze for a minute longer and then tucked her hair behind her ears, stepping back to lift Gabriel in his arms. "Hey, you, listen. You go with Jules to the kitchen because I bet you anything there is a fresh batch of cookies some-where down there. Am I right, Jules?"

Jules appeared to consider what he said. "I'm pretty sure Aida baked chocolate chip cookies yesterday, and I know there should be one or two left."

Andy put Gabriel down, and the boy took Jules' hand.

"Excuse me, Missus Friessen," Jules said as she tried to scoot past.

Caroline still hadn't moved, but she appeared irritated to have to step back and let Gabriel and Jules pass. Appar-ently, she also had no intention of leaving.

Andy sighed because he too knew Caroline was hovering like a pit bull just inside the doorway. "Come on, Laura, legs up." He plumped a pillow behind her. "I'll get more clothes and a nightgown for you to change into."

He sat beside her on the bed, resting his hip into and against her. Pressing both hands on either side of her, he leaned close. She could feel his warm breath and smell his scent, which was so appealing that she craved it. She would love nothing more than to lean in and smell him.

"Andy, you don't need to buy me new clothes. If you could just bring the bag up, there are perfectly good clothes in there, and a nightgown. They fit, and I won't be wearing them much longer, anyway."

"Laura, you're my wife. I don't want you wearing someone's castoffs. Don't fight me on this."

Laura could see that Caroline was still hovering in the doorway, with no intention of leaving. She wondered if the woman was listening to everything being said. Of course she was. Laura pressed her lips tightly and ducked her head, using Andy as her shield.

Andy must have known, as he glanced back at his mother and let out an irritated growl. "I'll be back in a minute." His big hand brushed her leg as he slid away, and she noticed his bare fingers. It stung again as she remembered his refusal to wear a ring. To her, it was a symbol of commitment, a way to tell every damn sexy women that he was taken and to stay far away from her man, a man she'd never admit how deeply she loved.

Caroline stepped into the hallway with Andy. "What are you doing, bringing her back here? I was told she was gone, and now she's pregnant. Are you out of your mind?" Caroline wasn't quiet, and, at times, she didn't care who heard her.

Even though Laura knew what kind of horrible woman she could be, it still hurt beyond belief to have anyone speak that way about her. She couldn't tear her eyes away from the door, and Andy noticed, as he pulled the door closed.

When someone was mean and hateful to her, the best thing to do was walk away. Laura knew that, but her legs seemed to be waging war with her common sense as they slid over the side of the bed and she walked as quietly as she could to the door. She could hear voices, Andy's deep baritone, sharp and cutting, and Caroline's, high and shrill. She pressed her ear closer to the door.

"My God, you know nothing about women. She's been gone for how long, and you bring her back here? How do you even know the baby's yours?"

Laura felt her face burn in rage. She wanted to rip open the door and yell at the woman that she wasn't a piece of trash.

"I am not discussing this with you. This is my business."

Laura couldn't make out what Caroline said next, but she heard Andy's voice clearer, closer to the door. "I need to check on my wife. I'll ask that you leave her alone."

Laura started back toward the bed and nearly jumped out of her skin when the door opened.

"What are you doing out of bed?" he barked. He had his hands on her by the time she turned around.

She couldn't lie for the life of her, and she felt lower than a dog for eavesdropping, but Andy didn't seem interested in waiting. He was distracted as he scooped her up again and set her on the bed.

"Stay. I'll grab the bag so you can change. I'll send Jules up, as well. I'll have her bring you something to eat and drink."

"Andy, I don't want to stay. Your mother doesn't want us here." She was touching his arm, where she could feel his triceps tighten beneath her touch.

He surrounded her with both arms, and, for the first time, pulled her into his chest. She rested her head against the solid wall of muscle, and he tucked her head under his chin and just held her.

"I want you to get some rest. Don't worry about my mother; I'll take care of her. The doctor's coming by as well later this afternoon. Laura, believe me when I say that

I won't let her hurt you and you're staying close to me. Listen, let me get Gabriel. I promised I'd take him on the horse with me, but I'll do it later."

The last thing she wanted was to disappoint Gabriel. He wanted to be with Andy, too, to go on the horse with him. She couldn't let him down.

"No, Andy, take Gabriel. I'll be fine."

He watched her intently and then slid his fingers into her hair at her scalp. He pressed a kiss into her forehead and stood up, standing by the bed for a second, his hands on those sexy hips. "Stay in bed."

He left, closing the door behind him, and, for the first time, Laura felt wanted.

CHAPTER

Twelve

Laura shifted on her side, nestled in a cocoon of pillows, one behind her back and one in front of her, where she rested her knee and cuddled the goose down into her swollen belly. She stared at the shadows of the late-day sun streaming in the window across the wall by Andy's side of the bed. She remembered, all too well, his touch, which had seemed so real to her. But it couldn't have been, after all they'd been through. If she wasn't pregnant with his babies, would he still be caring for her with this tenderness, which almost fooled her into believing he really cared about her? Did he have feelings for her? She wanted to believe she had found a way into his heart, but there were still things that unsettled her.

Dr. Richardson had been by earlier, and she was pleased with how Laura was doing. Her blood pressure was still high, and the doctor ordered her to stay in bed. Andy had given her a new cell phone and left it beside the bed so that she could call him or Jules whenever she needed something. It wasn't as if she could call out to anyone in a house this size, but she hated having anyone wait on her hand and foot.

Laura was thirsty, so she slid out of bed and searched Andy's closet for something to put on over her nightgown. She grabbed his black robe, slipped it on, and went down the stairs barefoot, holding the rail. The house was unusually quiet as she walked softly across the black and white tiled grand foyer toward the kitchen. She heard voices, a man's and Caroline's distinct clip coming from her dayroom.

"I want to make sure there is no problem getting those babies."

Laura felt her breath go out of her as if someone had rammed a fist into her gut. She pressed her hand to her swollen belly and stepped back against the wall on the other side of the grandfather clock. Who was Caroline talking to? She could hear a male voice but couldn't make it out. Was it Andy? Was he plotting with his mother to have her babies taken away?

"Look, you are the best attorney for these matters. I want to be sure that as soon as she has the babies, they'll be taken from her. No chance for her to see them. I want her gone, whatever you need to do to make it happen."

Panic came out of nowhere, and an ache ripped through her chest at the fear of having her children, her babies, taken from her. She knew she'd never survive that again. She gazed longingly at the front door from where she stood, which was maybe thirty feet away. How quickly could she get to it and start running?

Gabriel. Oh, shit. Where was he? She needed to find him, to leave and get as far away from Andy as she could.

Footsteps echoed on the tiled floor. There was not much she could do, so she stepped out behind the clock to where Caroline and a tall man dressed in a very expensive, dark suit, with glasses and short, reddish hair, stared at her. Caroline's mouth twisted as if she was disgusted with Laura.

The man with her cleared his throat. "Caroline, I'll speak with you tomorrow," he said, then stepped around Laura and left.

Caroline swept her icy gaze over Laura. Any two-year-old with a lick of common sense could pick up her meaning and what she thought of Laura. She hated her, and that worried Laura.

"Is Andy here?" Laura asked Caroline just as she turned her back and started toward her fancy dayroom. It had a glass desk and gleaming white and peach furnishings, a room Laura avoided mostly because of all the pristine white—she was afraid of leaving a mark anywhere.

Caroline was wearing a dusty blue Chanel suit that hugged her every curve. She stopped but didn't turn around as she said, "No, but I expect him shortly." Then she walked away.

Laura didn't know what to make of it. Okay, so Andy wasn't there, but had he talked to his mother about her? She needed to know. How would she ask him, and would he tell her the truth?

"What are you doing up?" Andy had pushed open the kitchen door, where voices and clatter trailed out. She could hear Gabriel chatting away to Aida.

"I was thirsty. I came down to get water." Laura started walking toward the kitchen and didn't miss the way his eyes took in what she was wearing. It was a look so intimate that a smile hinted at the side of his mouth. So he liked the fact that she was wearing his robe.

"It was all I could find to put on." She tried to slide past him and would have expected him to step back and make room, but he didn't, so her legs and hips and very large belly brushed him. He didn't appear to mind in the least. This was all very confusing for her, and she stared up at him for a minute, trying to read him, to figure him out.

"Are you okay?" he asked and then glanced around behind him. "Something happen? You look off."

Laura glanced into the kitchen, where Jules and two male servers were helping Aida. Laura stepped back.

"Jules, grab Laura some water bring it into the library," Andy said as he slid his arm around her back and walked her down the hall. In the library, he sat right beside her on the leather sofa, his legs pressing into her.

Laura squeezed the soft black robe between her fingers, because what she really wanted was to touch Andy, to touch his leg, to lean on him, but that would be a very bad idea. She was already sucked right back into loving him to the point that it was killing her inside. "Andy, did you talk to your mother about me, about the babies?"

"Yeah. I told her we're having twins. Did she say something to you?" He leaned closer to her, in her face, and was so close she could have touched her lips with his. She turned her head away, and he swept his fingers through her hair so that she was forced to look into his steely eyes, which were so strong she doubted he'd ever had a moment in his life when he was unsure of anything.

"Your mother had a man here. Do you know who it was?" She knew she wasn't saying much at all, but she felt as if she had been plunked into the middle of a cat and mouse game, and she was the mouse. Even though he could lie to her and she wouldn't have a clue whether he was telling the truth or not, she needed to ask.

Andy glanced up and over her head. "No, I didn't know. Is he still here?"

She shook her head. "No, he left."

"Well, I'm confused. Did he say something to you?"

Andy did in fact appear not to know, and she wondered for a minute what the hell was going on. But why would Caroline want anything to do with her babies?

"They were talking about my babies. I overheard Caroline with that man," Laura said as she pressed her hand into the small of her back and did her best to work out the tight knot that was making her damn uncomfortable.

Andy glanced up, but he had that look in his eyes that meant someone was irritating the hell out of him. "Who was the guy?"

"I don't know who it was, Andy."

"What did he look like, Laura?" Andy asked, but his eyes were staring straight out into the foyer as if he was considering something.

"Tall, reddish hair, glasses, wore a suit."

His gaze swiveled to her and appeared more than interested. He also seemed angry. "That would be her lawyer, it sounds like. What exactly did you hear?"

Okay, maybe he didn't know, because he really was acting as if there was something not quite right. "Your mother said she was taking my babies away from me as soon as I had them so I'd have no chance to see them."

Andy jammed both hands through his dark, tousled hair, which was still a windblown mess. He opened his mouth as if to say something and bit down hard with his jaw. She could tell he was so mad that he was grinding his teeth. Then he blew out a heated breath, much as a bull does before it charges. He opened his fisted hands and took another breath, trying to calm down. He picked her hand up and pried it from his housecoat until she allowed him to hold it, and she watched him doing his damnedest to pull it together before speaking.

"Laura..."

"You shouted at me that you were going to take them

away," she interrupted, because she too was burning with rage. She didn't want to stay in this uncomfortable house one minute longer. "So tell me, Andy, is this the plan? Get me back here and then, as soon as I have the babies, use your money and power to toss me out in the street and take them?"

"No!" he shouted. "And we already talked about this. I was angry because you hid them from me. I thought we were done with this. I thought you'd moved past it."

"Well, evidently not. Or rather, after what I heard from your mother..."

"She has no say in what we do," he barked out before she could finish. "No, I would never do something like that. My God, what kind of monster do you think I am? You must have heard wrong, Laura."

She tried to pull her hand from his, but he held tight, and the second time she yanked harder and pulled free. "No, I did not. I may have heard only one side, but I heard your mother clearly." Laura struggled to her feet. "I don't want to stay here. I can't be worried about that."

Andy was on his feet right beside her. "Whoa, wait a second. You're overreacting. One, you're not giving me credit. Do you think I'd let my mother take our babies? Not going to happen, Laura. Come on, let me get you back to bed."

He didn't let her stay and argue. His arm was around her, and he led her upstairs and back into their room. "Look, dinner's almost done. I'll have Jules bring dinner up here for all of us. Gabriel and me, we'll camp up here with you, have dinner together."

Laura allowed him to help her on the bed. She loved the feel of his hands on her. She wanted to believe him, she needed to, because she wanted him so badly that it ached in every part of her to think he'd betray her. She didn't want to leave him; she wanted to believe he had changed, because he had the ability to hold her heart in the palm of his large, sexy hand and crush it.

He slid his hands over her shoulders and then tucked her sleep-tousled hair behind her ears. "You're over-thinking again."

"Andy, I want to trust you, but with what your mother said, you and I both know how powerful she is and what she's capable of."

"Laura, stop. I'll handle my mother. Look, just take a breath." He shook his head as if annoyed at her and glanced away. She could feel his wall come up again. He was so good at shutting her out. When he faced her this time, his entire expression was annoyed and appeared as if he was doing everything he could not to snap at her. "I don't know what it's going to take, Laura, to get you to trust me. Tell me."

"I want to move out of here. Can you find us a small place, nothing this big, but something away from your mother? I don't want any servants, just us." She held her breath, wondering what he'd say. She had put herself out there, hoping he wouldn't dismiss her idea and that he wanted to build a life with her, but the truth was that even though she wanted him so badly, she was afraid his feelings for her weren't real.

"Laura, this is our home. My mother won't be here long. She'll be off soon to one of our other houses."

"This is not my home, Andy. I'm not comfortable with all this." She gestured to the room, everything lavish and expensive in it.

Andy cupped her face with his one hand and made her look at him. "You're my wife. This will be all mine; it's my birthright, and it's the way we Friessens do things. I am the only son, and this is all passed to me, and I'll pass it on to my son. We're not leaving here. You're going to stay in bed and relax. I'll protect you. You have to trust me, Laura."

This time, he didn't wait for her to answer. He stood up, and she could tell he was annoyed, as he raked his hands through his hair. "Look, we're both tired...."

A knock on the open door interrupted Andy.

They both stared at Jules, who was standing awkwardly in the doorway. "The water for Laura." She held up a tray with a pitcher and two glasses.

"Just set it down." Andy gestured to the side table in between the two chairs by the fireplace. "Oh, and could you have dinner sent up here? Gabriel and I are going to eat here with Laura."

"Of course, sir." Jules set the water down. "Is there anything else you need in the meantime?" Jules glanced at Laura, but it was Andy she asked.

"No. I'll come down and grab Gabriel."

Andy poured a glass of water, and Jules hurried out the door. He handed Laura the glass, and she sipped at the water.

"Thank you," she said, then set it on the bedside table beside her. "Andy..."

He cut her off. "No, Laura, let's just have dinner with Gabriel, get a good night's sleep. I know you'll feel differently in the morning. It's just the stress of the day."

He did look tired, and she was frazzled. Maybe he was right.

She shut her eyes and sighed. When she looked back up at him, she said, "Okay, but will you talk with me tomorrow about this and not blow me off?"

If a man could be exasperated by a woman, the expression on Andy's face was exactly that. "Oh, for the love of God, Laura. I will deal with my mother. A week, Laura, give it a week. I assure you my mother will most likely be gone and I'm sure you'll feel differently by then, too. But we'll talk then, okay?" He waited for her to respond. Frankly, he wasn't being unreasonable.

"All right, one week."

He didn't exactly smile at her, but his expression softened. "I'll grab Gabriel and be right back."

He left, looking so damn good from behind. She knew this man could talk her into anything if she let him, especially when he looked at her the way he did. If she wasn't careful, he'd be organizing and planning her life, and she couldn't allow him to do that, not ever again.

CHAPTER
Thirteen

"Is Gabriel asleep?" Laura strode out of the bathroom, her damp hair brushed back, wearing Andy's robe again and nothing underneath.

"Yeah, with a smile on his face." Andy sat on his side of the bed and unbuttoned his shirt.

Laura froze and stared at his incredible chest and the dark hair that lightly covered it. He stood up and walked straight for her, and she felt her face heat and probably turn a nice shade of red.

"Laura, you better get used to this, because I'm not changing in the bathroom." He chuckled under his breath and slid his hand behind her neck, his other in her wet hair, and he leaned down. She swore he was about to kiss her, he was so close. He touched his nose to hers, and she couldn't help breathing in how he smelled. It was earthy, and, good God, made her knees weak. His scent was indescribable and all man, her man.

"I need a shower," he said and went to pull back, but Laura reached her hand up and slid it over his whiskered cheek.

"You smell so good."

He smiled his sexy smile and touched his lips to hers, and she couldn't stop the tremble that shot through her, making her weak in the knees. He must have known, as he slid his arm inside the housecoat. She couldn't think how he managed to untie it so easily as he caressed her belly, the small of her back, sliding his rough hand over her bare skin, running his thumb under her breast and his other around her bottom as he used his tongue to deepen the kiss, tasting her until she was taking his breath as hers.

Andy caressed her rounded cheek, touching her so she lifted her leg up to hook around his hip. Her large belly poked into him, and he pulled away, grabbing her as his bathrobe fell open wide and she was naked before him.

"I'm sorry. I didn't mean to get so carried away." He was breathing hard, but she doubted he was anywhere near as out of breath as she was.

Laura went to pull the housecoat closed in front, but Andy stopped her. "No, wait. I want to see you. My God, you're beautiful." He slid his hand over her large belly, running his other hand up her side and over her breasts, which had grown throughout her pregnancy. He placed his palms over both of her nipples and watched her as he ran his hands over her breasts in a circle.

Laura held on to his arms and could feel his control as his muscles flexed under her touch. For a moment, she felt safe. He leaned down slowly again to taste her, to touch his lips to hers, and she wanted him so much that a moan slipped out just as his lips covered hers and she opened for him. He pulled his lips away, resting his forehead against hers.

"I've got to stop now."

"What if I don't want you to stop?" She licked her lips

as she watched his heavy gaze and the sizzle that deepened the blue ring of his iris. God, how she loved his eyes.

"No, not until I talk to the doctor and find out if its safe." This time, he stepped back, and when she grabbed the edge of his housecoat to close it again, he put his hands over hers. "I love to look at you. Don't hide yourself."

She couldn't help the warmth that rocketed through her center. "I'm not very attractive right now."

"Oh, that's where you're wrong." He slid his hands over her shoulders until she relaxed and just stood before him. "Get in bed. I'll be right there. I'm going to grab a shower, a cold one, I think."

He was halfway to the bathroom when she finally said, "Andy, I don't have a clean nightgown. Those clothes that arrived earlier, there was no nightgown in there."

He smiled and rested his arm above his head on the door jam. "Yeah, I know," he said, and then he disappeared. A second later, she heard the shower pop on.

Laura perched on her side of the bed, still wearing Andy's bathrobe. She loved the feel of the silky material and the fact that he'd worn it. She could smell his scent in it, and she didn't want to take it off, but the thought of sleeping naked with Andy, taking off the robe and slipping under the covers now with nothing on, pressed against her husband—oh, she wanted to do it. She dreamed of having the courage, but she'd never been as comfortable in her own body as he was, strutting around as if it were the most natural thing.

"Are you going to sit there all night, or are you going to get in bed?" Andy came to stand in front of Laura, a towel wrapped loosely around his hips. How long had she been sitting their, day dreaming?

All Laura could do was shake her head as she stood on

shaky legs and slid his robe off, tossing it to the foot of the bed and pulling back the covers to climb in.

Andy, of course, watched her every move closely, his eyes filled with heat. He reached for his robe and tossed it across the room, where it landed on one of the chairs. The towel soon followed. He didn't just stride in his cocky way, fully erect, around to his side of the bed; he watched her as she lay on her side and faced him, and he pulled her into his arms. She rested her head on his chest and ran her hand down to touch him, but he grabbed her hand.

"Not a good idea."

"I feel fine."

He pressed a kiss to her forehead. "Yeah, well, I don't, and I'm not taking any chances until I talk to the doctor. So go to sleep."

"Sleep? Are you kidding, Andy? I'm not tired. I've been in bed all day."

He ran his hand over her head, smoothing down her hair, and then down her back, tracing tiny circles in her lower back. She kissed his chest and wondered how much control he had, as being in bed with Andy had always meant him taking her as his. She knew he had a healthy sexual appetite, and, right now, she wanted him, to connect with him, have him inside her, just to feel again.

He started to pull away.

"Where are you going?" she asked?

"To take another cold shower."

CHAPTER

Fourteen

L aura felt far from rested, snuggled in Andy's very comfortable, large bed. Andy had been gone when she finally woke late in the morning after a long restless night. Even after his cold shower, she could feel how tight he was as he held her and how much he wanted her still.

Now it was almost lunchtime, and Laura was settled in bed, wearing a peach-colored maternity tracksuit, which was very comfortable. The price tag that was attached had nearly given her a coronary. She couldn't believe what Andy tossed away on clothes, even though it was the most comfortable outfit she'd worn in months.

Dr. Richardson ripped off the black cuff. "Well, your blood pressure is better." She folded it up and tucked it into her bag, pulling out her Doppler to listen to the babies' heartbeats just as Andy pushed the door open and strode in, looking sexy in his dark jeans and white t-shirt. He had shaved.

"How's she doing?" He didn't stop until he was

standing beside the bed, watching over Laura. His hair was brushed but a little on the longish side.

"Blood pressure is good. Just about to check the heartbeats."

Laura scooted down on her back and pulled up her shirt. "Could you hurry? This is really uncomfortable."

The doctor squirted a bit of that cool jelly on Laura's bare abdomen and pressed the white Doppler to a few places on her large belly, searching for a heartbeat. It didn't take long for one to register. "There's one. Hear that? Wow, nice and strong."

Andy was grinning ear to ear, and for the first time ever, his eyes softened and shimmered with a joy she'd never seen before. My God, he was going to love those babies. How could she ever have considered hiding them? She was ashamed and had to look away.

"There's the other, nice and strong, too." The doctor turned up the volume so the only thing Laura could hear in the room was the echo and beat of the babies' hearts. The sound made it so real.

"We should talk about delivery options, especially with twins. Have you two talked about what to expect?" The doctor used a small hand towel to wipe off the jelly.

Laura yanked her cotton maternity shirt down and scooted up as the doctor shoved a couple pillows behind her back. She couldn't read the look in Andy's eyes. "We haven't talked about anything like that, but I'd like to know when I can get out of bed. There are some other things we wanted to ask you, too." Laura felt her face heat and had to look down at her hands as she heard Andy's chuckle. The bed sank a little beside her as he sat right next to her and took her hand in his.

"Doc, I want to know about sex. Is it completely out of the question, or is it safe?"

Laura groaned and grabbed his arm, wanting to bury her head into his wide chest and hide.

"Oh, I see," Dr. Richardson said with a hint of humor in her voice. "Well, for now, as long as you take it easy and don't do anything rough, it should be okay, but if you feel any discomfort, stop."

Laura couldn't look at the doctor, but she did smile shyly at Andy and sensed that he wanted nothing more than to walk the doc out, shut the door and have his way with her right now. That was fine with her.

The doctor cleared her throat. "Okay, you two, its good to see you resolved some things and that you're back home, Laura. Now let's talk about the babies' delivery. Have you two talked about natural, drug, epidural, and what's involved with delivering twins?"

"I don't want to do drugs, Andy."

He just watched her and didn't take his eyes off her when he spoke to the doctor. "Can you walk us through what to expect? Laura doesn't want to do drugs, but I don't want her hurting, either."

Oh, boy, was he ever saying the right things, and, for the first time, she felt her heart softening and leaping to the moon at the thought that maybe her prince charming more than just cared for her. That inkling of a happily ever after with Andy had her heart so full she though it would burst.

"Well, with twins, it's hard to tell. You're having two babies, so double everything, and it can take a while after you've had the first before you dilate again to have the second. That's if we don't have to do a C-section, if everything goes well. There are options, and I suggest that you start a prenatal class, one that also walks you through labor and delivery so you can learn breathing and what you can do, Andy, to help Laura through her labor. Don't get stuck on a birth plan, because just about every couple who's outlined one has to toss it out the window come labor. I don't want you to be disappointed. Just know your options." She dug a booklet out and handed it to Andy. "Read up, and if you have questions, just ask. Also, you'll note Debra Kirk's name and number on the last page. She's a labor coach who runs a class. I suggest you call her."

"Thanks, Doc." Andy leafed through the booklet and then handed it to Laura. "Looks like we have some reading to do."

Laura frowned as she glanced at the twenty-page booklet. She didn't remember being offered anything like this when she had Gabriel, but, then again, she'd been pregnant at fifteen and barely turned sixteen when she'd gone into labor alone, with no help, at a county hospital, pumped with drugs, screaming and crying. It had been a horrible experience.

"Hey, it's all right." Andy's hand was covering hers, which now squeezed the booklet and was shaking.

"You'll be with me?" She needed to know. She needed to hear him say it, even though she couldn't imagine him not being there. She didn't want to go through this alone even though she had been very much prepared to do so before he showed up again. The fact was that she wanted him there.

"I'm not letting you do this alone. We'll do it as a team."

The doctor cleared her throat again. "Well, unless you have any other questions, I will let myself out."

"Doctor Richardson, can I get out of bed? Please tell me I don't have to stay cooped up here in this room, because I am getting really bored," Laura asked.

"Well, I'll tell you what—you can if you promise to

take it easy, no brisk walks, getting up only to eat. Spend most of the day resting, no lifting or bending." The doctor took in both Andy and Laura with her stern gaze.

"She'll spend most of the day in bed, resting, Doc. You have my word," Andy said in a way that let Laura catch his meaning.

"Well, okay then. I'll be by tomorrow, same time. I'll see myself out."

The door shut behind the doctor, and Laura sucked her bottom lip in between her teeth and slid her hands up Andy's arms, which were still planted on either side of her. He took a deep breath and let it out in a way that sounded more like a groan, then leaned closer and kissed her, softly at first as she opened and he tasted her, deepening the kiss. She felt herself getting pulled into him, and she wrapped her arms around his neck as he slid his hand up and over her breast, which was throbbing. She moaned into his mouth.

Then the door banged open.

"Andy, Andy, Mommy!"

Andy pulled back. Laura was dizzy and stunned as Gabriel leaped across the room and landed on Andy.

"Oh, sir, and Laura, I'm sorry he got away from me." Jules was standing in the open doorway, and Andy wrestled a giggling Gabriel at the foot of the bed, tickling him.

"Jules, I've got him," Andy said as he quirked his brow at Laura. "Well, I think I better wear this big guy out so he's tired and in bed early tonight. What do you think?"

Laura sighed because she didn't think she'd ever get tired of hearing Gabriel laugh and giggle the way he did with Andy. Gabriel loved him.

Andy tossed Gabriel over his shoulder and stood up. "Don't race any marathons. Better yet, stay in bed. I want you well rested for tonight."

He left, and, this time, when he shut the door, her heart swelled. She didn't leap out of bed but sighed, realizing she was a goner. Her heart was full, tender, and vulnerable because she loved him, too. She stared at the ceiling, wondering what she was going to do when there was a soft knock on the door.

"Come in," Laura said. She waited as the door opened and Aida stepped in, wearing her blue and white apron over her black dress. She was still wearing her hairnet.

"Laura, I just came up to see how you are." Aida stood there in the doorway, holding the doorknob and glancing around as if she shouldn't be there.

"Aida, I am so glad you came up here. Please come in." She patted the spot beside her on the mattress and watched as Aida shut the door and strode across the room to her, taking in the gold trim and all the expensive furnishings in the room.

"Andy gave me more money. I had it stuffed in my purse for you." She reached her wrinkled, bony hand into her apron pocket and handed a wad of cash to Laura. "I didn't count it, but any fool can see it's a lot of money."

Laura reached for the folded bills, thick and heavy, and set them on the bedside table.

"Are you back here because you want to be, girl?" Aida asked.

When Laura stared back at the old cook, who'd been like a mother to her, she let out a heavy sigh. "I love him, and I wasn't being fair, keeping him from his babies, not telling him."

"No, you weren't, but I told you that. I'm just glad you see it. He's not a monster, Laura, and no man worries and hands cash over to someone he barely knows to give it to his wife who's all but disappeared so she can buy food, pay rent. Only a man who cares does that." Aida didn't sit on the bed. She did, though, stand right beside the bed, looking down on Laura. It was the first time Laura noticed how tired the old woman looked.

"Are you okay, Aida? I mean, you look so tired. Is everything all right?"

"Oh, posh tosh, I'm fine. Just my knees aching a little bit lately. Don't worry about me but I need to know if you're staying and what you're doing. Is Andy treating you okay? Are you still going to divorce him? What about Gabriel? I've been watching those two together since Andy brought you two back here yesterday. He loves that boy, and Gabby worships him. You can't come between that, Laura."

"I know, Aida. I never realized how much Andy cared for Gabriel. I guess I never paid attention, because when Andy showed up yesterday, Gabriel was in his arms, he wouldn't let him go, and he looked to Andy to keep him safe, protect him, and not to me. I don't know what to do, Aida. I just know I don't ever want to be treated like nothing again." She stared at Aida, who firmed her lips and nodded as if deciding something.

"Then you need to make sure he respects you. You set the ground rules. You may be young, but you have common sense. You also need to decide with Andy what's best for you and him, him and Gabriel, and both you and the babies. Do you want a life without Andy?"

Laura already knew the answer to that, and Aida had a way of cutting right through the bullshit. She had never once told her what to do. She listened without judgment and told her flat out when someone was doing something right or wrong. She never took it on herself, and Laura knew that whatever secrets she kept, she'd take them to her grave. Aida had a look about her as if she carried a lot of people's secrets, and maybe a few of her own.

"Yes, I want a family with Andy. I want a life with him. I want him to be a father to Gabriel, and I want him to love me."

"Well, then. Sounds to me as if you've figured out a few things. Knowing what you really want is all good, and all that sounds more than reasonable, so don't settle for anything less than all of it." This time, Aida pressed her hand to Laura's forehead and then brushed her hair back. "Don't underestimate how that man feels about you. You are not powerless here, not in any of this, so its time you and your husband got to know each other, don't you think?" Aida patted her arm and then hurried to the bedroom door. "Just one thing, Laura. When dealing with a man like Andy Friesian, you can't push him. You need to let him in."

Laura watched the closed door after Aida left and pressed her hand over her battered and bruised heart. She wondered if she'd have the courage to ever allow someone completely in.

CHAPTER
Fifteen

Laura didn't think she could get any bigger, and if anyone had told her six weeks ago that she'd get a lot bigger yet, she'd have thought they were kidding. She'd long since lost the ability to see her feet, so, as she climbed on the scale in the morning, she was now using a hand mirror to see her weight.

"What are you doing?" Andy strode in the bathroom butt naked, his hair sticking up, and yawned.

"I gained another two pounds." Laura set the mirror down and stepped off the scale, glimpsing herself in the bathroom mirror, horrified at her size and by how much she looked like a beached whale. "I'm huge, and I want my waistline back, and my back hurts.... Sorry, I don't mean to complain." She sighed, and Andy stepped behind her and slid his arms around her naked front. She could still feel the twinges of him inside her as he woke her this morning. It was erotic and hot and...

"What are you thinking about?" He nuzzled her neck and trailed his lips over her ear, and she leaned back into him, feeling him, loving him. It was so much like a honey-moon, the one they never had. She watched him in the mirror as she leaned into him and felt all his hardness pressed against her.

"You." She smiled at him in the mirror as he ran his hands over her huge belly, and she placed hers over his with a flash of the diamond band he'd given her just last week, signifying she was his. She glimpsed his bare finger and frowned.

"Laura, what is it?"

She met his deep gaze in the mirror. Lord, he was so strong, every part of him: his mind, his body, his will. "When are you going to wear a wedding ring?"

"I'm not. I don't wear rings, Laura." He went to pull away, but she grabbed his arm, and he appeared annoyed. "Why do you want me to wear a ring, anyway?"

He pulled away, and so did she, wanting to cover herself. She hated when he got like this; it made her feel inadequate. He must have known, because he scooped his finger under her chin, lifting it up.

"Don't do that. Don't pull into yourself."

She frowned. "Andy, I want you to wear a ring so that you can tell every one of those tarts who throws herself at you that I'm your wife." She grabbed his hand. "A wedding ring tells every one of those women to piss off because your mine and they can't have you." She let go of his hand. "That's why," she snapped and then turned away, striding out of the bathroom. She was halfway across the room when he scooped her up, and she shrieked as he laid her on the bed, resting a pillow under her head just as he slid inside her and she gasped.

He held himself above her, his muscles flexing in his arms. The dark, predator-like caveman face that he had when he claimed her hovered inches from hers, and he touched her lips with his and moved. "Well, baby, just so you know, you are right about one thing. You are mine, every last inch of you." He punctuated that point long and hard as he drove himself into her again and again until she lay moaning and gasping, uncomfortable as all hell but not wanting him to stop. She felt it building, the power of him and what he did to her, and that had her crying out his name as she felt his warmth spill into her.

It was impossible for him to collapse on top of her, so he pulled away and moved her onto her side. He curled up behind her, pressing into her, and she reached her hand back and ran it over his tight ass.

"Wow, that was..."

"Amazing. Awesome," Andy said. "Is that what you were going to say?"

"Yeah, that's what I was going to say, all right." She played with his fingers, lacing hers with his, loving the feel of his large, calloused hands and how they touched every inch of her.

He kissed her shoulder, her neck. "I'm still not wearing a ring, but I'm thinking about adding one to yours." He slid off the bed and strode in that cocky walk of his into the bathroom. "What time is the doctor coming today, Laura?" he called out.

"Just after lunch, around one. Are you going to be here?" She heard the toilet flush and the water running. Then he leaned in the doorway.

"I am, but we have that last class with Debra first, I thought. I think it starts in an hour." He watched her across the room with those brilliant blue eyes that had brightened, she swore, to a lighter blue over the last few weeks. "Do you want to join me for a shower?"

She scooted off the bed about as gracefully as a woman pregnant with twins could. "Yes, I do." She waddled straight toward him and allowed him to run his gaze over all of her. Laura, for the first time, loved it.

CHAPTER

Sixteen

Laura had just woken up from a late-morning nap after meeting with Debra and going over some of the things to be expected at the hospital. She had explained that labor progressed fast or slow, never the same, and it was something that could never be predicted. Did she want an epidural? Did she want drugs that tapped the surface of the pain? There was only a small window to use them, and with twins, after the first, it was expected that her cervix would shrink down and she'd have to dilate again for the second. Everything came down to Andy as her support, getting her through labor, each stage, breathing and keeping her relaxed. It was terrifying and exciting all at once, and Andy was the one asking all of the questions. He was also the one making the plans, arranging for a private birthing room at the hospital where they'd go when she went into labor. For the first time, Laura had stopped worrying.

She glanced at the bedside clock; eleven thirty—she'd only slept an hour. She wanted to go into the kitchen and have a word with Aida before lunch. She hadn't had much time over the past few weeks to spend time and just see how she was doing. She was, in fact, worried about Aida. She was the kindest older woman she'd ever met, and she'd never once judged Laura, taking her in, providing her and Gabriel a bed and shelter, and letting her cry every night for months without once saying "I told you so."

Laura was still wearing the maternity jeans and bright green and pink paisley shirt that were among the dozens and dozens of outfits that Andy kept buying for her. She'd told him to stop, but he hadn't, and she was positive she'd never be able to wear them all. She glanced at her image in the mirror. She had dark smudges under both eyes, and she was starting to wonder if they'd always be there. She ran a brush through her hair and then started down the stairs, holding the rail and taking her time, as she couldn't see where her feet were stepping. When she reached the bottom, she had started toward the kitchen when she heard a familiar voice and stopped. It took her a second to place the soft, pleasant voice of Dr. Richardson. She was early, and Laura was eager to talk to her about what Debra had shared at their last birthing class and listen to her babies' heartbeats again, so she started waddling toward her with a smile on her face. She froze when she heard Caroline's sharp voice, and something inside her heart thunked. All her joy with Andy crumbled, bringing an awful ache inside her.

"Yes or no is all I want to know. Is it safe for her to have the babies now?"

"It would be best if she made it three more weeks. The babies' lungs are still developing."

"Three more weeks with that piece of trash under my roof."

Laura stood humbly beside the grandfather clock and

listened to Caroline sigh in the annoyed way she did when she couldn't deal with something and it had to go.

"Well, I guess that's a small price until my son can be rid of her. It's becoming difficult, keeping a straight face and remaining pleasant. I don't know how Andy does it so well, but, then again, he does take after his father in so many ways."

Laura's hand was trembling as she pressed it to her heart. Her eyes burned, and it was only a matter of time before the tears streamed down her cheeks and she wouldn't be able to stop them. It was one of those moments when she knew someone had just yanked the rug right out from under her and she'd landed hard on her backside. She could even feel the ache in her back as if it were already battered and bruised.

"After I do the C-section, she'll be out for a while, so she won't see the babies. Do you have everything ready for the twins?" It was the doctor again who asked. That nice woman who said she couldn't and wouldn't break confidentiality, that she was her doctor. Apparently, she had lied, and in such a sincere way, too.

"I've already hired a nanny, and the nursery's done. Everything is handled here, so when those babies come home, they will be in competent hands. My son will not have to worry that his babies aren't being cared for, and then he can get on with finding someone more suitable. I have just the woman in mind."

"The mother will probably ask to hold her babies when she wakes up."

Laura couldn't believe what she was hearing. Were they going to see that she disappeared? Could a doctor do a C-section just like that and take her babies from her? This was criminal, what they were planning, and at that moment every good thing she felt for Andy turned to ashes. She could hear footsteps and pressed her back to the wall until she heard the women pass on the other side of the clock, heading toward the dining room at the far end of the house.

Laura slipped away and hurried up the stairs, her hand over her babies, who were still part of her, inside her. She didn't know what she was looking for but started down the long hallway, opening doors and peeking in. She turned the corner to Caroline's wing, and when she opened the third door, her heart cracked open like a steel vault. Tears filled her eyes as she stepped into a nursery with two cradles, change tables, a rocker, a daybed. The room was filled corner to corner with stuffed animals, white and lavender everywhere. It was for her babies, and at that moment she couldn't bring herself to touch one thing, as she felt so betrayed by Andy. She wished she could hate him, the man to whom she'd handed her heart on a platter, the man who'd pretended to care for her, to love her so passionately for weeks. Even just a few hours ago, he'd taken her on his bed, but obviously to him it was just sex, all a game. She pressed her back to the wall and wept as soundlessly as she could as her legs gave way and she slid down to the floor, pressing her hand to her mouth, choking on her sobs.

She didn't know how long she sat there in a crumpled heap, struggling to breath, with all her energy gone. When she felt the baby's foot in her side and another on her bladder, she scrambled on her knees and struggled to her feet. She swiped her face and her nose with her sleeve, then grabbed a few Kleenex from one of the boxes and blew her nose, stuffing the tissue in her pocket. Her face felt tight and swollen, and her eyes burned. When she caught her image in one of the gilded mirrors in the room, her face was red and blotchy, her eyes swollen and filled with those red lines that meant she had cried a thousand tears.

But she couldn't do anything about it as she pulled the door open and peeked out, leaving the fancy nursery. She was halfway down the hall to her bedroom when she heard footsteps on the stairs and Andy's voice. Her heart started hammering, and she froze for a minute, looking for a place to hide, but then he was in front of their open door, that bitch of a doctor with him. Laura jammed her mouth shut, grinding her teeth, wanting to scream and yell and pound her fists into him. But that would be a damn stupid thing to do, because she'd give herself away and let him know what a despicable monster she thought he was.

"Laura, what are you doing there?" Andy was in front of her. "Are you okay?" He even appeared concerned.

She really was an idiot, and she wondered if he had to leave the room just to have a good laugh every day at how he'd played her. When he touched her cheek, she flinched.

"What happened? What's going on?" he snapped, and she glanced at the fury and something else in his gaze that confused her.

She looked away and did something she never did. "Nothing, I'm sorry. I just had a bad dream. I have to go pee." She hurried as fast as she could into Andy's bedroom and to the bathroom and shut the door. She had to pull it together, but she was physically ill at the thought that this woman was going to put her hands on her and she was going to let her. She had to get through this exam, then get this woman the hell away from her. And Gabriel, where was he? She had to find him and figure out a way to disappear. Forever.

She flushed the toilet, washed her hands, and splashed cool water over her face again and again, then wiped it.

She still looked a mess, but the tap on the door nearly sent her through the roof.

"Laura." He turned the locked doorknob, clicking it back and forth. "Laura, open the door."

She turned the lock and opened it, and there he stood, staring at her with that dark look. The man was no fool; he knew something was going on, and if she wasn't careful, she'd spill it, or he'd read everything on her face. She was as transparent as a piece of plastic wrap, so she rested her hand on her large belly and said, "I didn't realize I had locked it. Sorry, I feel kind of odd with the doctor in our bedroom. Isn't she early?"

"Yeah, I ran into her downstairs. I thought you told me she was coming after lunch." Andy slid his arm around Laura's shoulders, and she did everything she could not to shrink away.

The doctor had set her bag down, but she didn't look up at Laura until she sat on the bed. "All right, are you ready to have a listen to these babies?"

Laura forced a smile to her face, but it ached so much that it had to look phony, so she glanced at her fingers and had to blink back tears as she stared at the diamond wedding band glittering from her finger.

"Laura, you don't look all right. What's going on?" Andy sat right beside her and slid both of his hands on her arms, and she knew that unless she got him to move away, she'd start screaming.

"I'm just so tired, Andy. I really just want to lie down and go to sleep." She refused to look at him, and she could feel him studying her. He had coiled up like a snake, pulling away.

When she glanced up at the doctor, she was watching her closely in a way that had Laura's alarm bells going off. She was really screwing this up. The last thing she wanted was to tip anyone off to what she'd heard. At this point, the babies, her babies, were still safely inside of her, and she needed to find a way to get Andy and the doctor to leave without suspecting her concerns, because she didn't know what either of them had planned. She considered both of them capable of anything, so she slid her shirt up and scooted down, allowing the doctor to squirt jelly on her tummy. When the babies' heartbeats echoed through the room, she shut her eyes and listened.

She pretended to be asleep when Andy came in. She had tucked the covers under her chin so he couldn't see that she was dressed in the peach sweat suit. The last thing she wanted was him touching her or trying to take her clothes off. She knew he would have just put Gabriel to bed, and it took everything she had to keep her breathing even as he stood over her. He ran his hand over her shoulder and lifted strands of her hair, running his fingers through it. Then he pulled away, and the floor squeaked as he stepped back. Her breath caught, and he said, "I know you're awake, and I don't know what's going on with you, Laura, but I thought we were past this."

A tear slipped out, and she squeezed her eyes shut, her face scrunching up as the power of the emotions she had struggled all day to bottle up broke away. Andy, being Andy, leaned over her, his strong arms boxing her in on her side, his face hovering just inches from hers. She couldn't stop the hysterics as she started choking with her tears, and then he was beside her on the bed, pulling her up into his arms.

"Laura, what's wrong, honey?" He rested his chin on top of her head and wrapped his arms around her back, rubbing up and down as she buried her face against his chest, squeezing her fists into his dark shirt and shaking her head.

She didn't know how long he held her, and she mourned what was to come. The thought that she might never feel his arms around her again was killing her, but knowing it was all a lie gave her the strength to push away.

"Laura, I've never seen you like this. Something has upset you. Why won't you tell me what it is? Did my mother say something to you?"

She flinched, and he slid his hand over her shoulder.

"So it was my mother. What did she do this time?"

She couldn't look at him. "Andy, I'm tired. I just want to get some sleep. Please." She waited, but the man didn't move.

He reached to caress her cheek, and she saw his hand come up and then stop as he squeezed it and pulled away. "Okay, get some sleep, but I want you to talk to me about this tomorrow."

Laura went to scoot back down on her side under the covers.

"Laura, let me help you get undressed."

"No, Andy, please. I'm cold. Just let me rest like this," she snapped, and she hoped he'd just leave and not push it as he usually did.

He let out a sigh she knew well. He probably wanted to reach out and shake her, but he didn't. He stood up and pulled the covers over her, leaned down to kiss her cheek, and paused for a second. He kissed her cheek again. "I'll come back and check on you in a bit."

"Is Gabriel asleep?" She didn't look at Andy when she asked and held her breath, waiting for his answer.

"He should be. He was really tired. I took him riding again. He really loves it, Laura. You should've see his face when I put him on Sugar in the round ring—he had her backing up all by himself today."

She rolled over on her back and was stunned by the hurt and love and something else in his eyes. Then she rolled on her side and gave him her back again. "Goodnight, Andy."

She hated him now for pretending to care for Gabriel and plotting with his mother and the doctor to rip her babies away. She waited for the click of the door, and then she sat up and struggled to the edge of the bed, listening to Andy's footsteps on the stairs. She hurried to the door and opened it quietly, peeking out. She could hear him in the foyer, speaking with someone, and then listened to his footsteps, imagining he'd gone into his library, as he did every night, for a drink, to make some calls and catch up on whatever big project he was working on. Whatever it was, she didn't have a clue.

Laura shivered in her thin t-shirt and tiptoed to their huge walk-in closet. She grabbed a dark sweater that still had its price tag dangling, ripped the tag off, and pulled it on. She grabbed the brand new pair of sneakers from the shoe rack and sat on the chair, struggling to pull them on and tie them as best she could. Then she slipped out of the bedroom, pulling the door closed behind her and walking as quietly as she could down the empty hall to Gabriel's room, two doors down. She slipped inside, shutting the door behind her, and watched over her little boy, who was sound asleep. How was she going to get him out of the house without him making any noise? She slid his closet open and pulled his sneakers and a hoodie out, then grabbed a pair of socks from the chest of drawers.

She slid the covers back and put his socks on, and when

he stirred and started whining, Laura sat him up and slid his coat on.

"No, Mommy, tired."

"I know, Gabriel. I have a surprise for you, and I need you to be very quiet. We're going on an adventure, and then you can go to sleep. Please, honey, I need you to be very quiet. We're going to pretend we're sneaking out of the castle of the wicked witch."

Gabriel rubbed his eyes as Laura slipped his shoes on and tied the laces. "Andy come?" he said.

"He's going to meet us, but we have to be very quiet." She felt lower than a dung beetle for lying to her child. It was despicable. She hated herself and prayed that Gabriel would forgive her, but he didn't see the monster that Andy was, and she despised Andy for that. A man who hurt women, who hurt children and used them for his own means, was truly a monster, and that was who they were running from.

"Shh. Remember, quiet as a mouse. So, my little prince, is there a secret door out of this castle where we can sneak out so no one can see us? A magic door?" She knew there was a back door from the kitchen and one at the end of the hall by Caroline's wing.

Gabriel rubbed his eyes and said nothing.

Laura held Gabriel's hand as she opened the door just a crack and peeked out, listening for any footsteps. When she heard nothing, she glanced down at Gabriel and said, "Remember, quiet as a mouse." Then she opened the door, stepping out and hurrying down the hall to the end, where the outside door led to the back steps. She turned the dead bolt and opened the door, praying that it wasn't hooked up to an alarm, and then hurried down as fast as she could with Gabriel in the dark, unable to see any of the steps. At the bottom, they stepped onto the grass. The lights from inside the house cut through the shadows of the darkness as the sun set and night fell.

"Mommy, I'm cold. I want see Andy."

Oh, crap. She knew he could get really loud. "Andy is going to meet us. We have to go to the trail in the woods first. Come on, let's go."

She hurried, which was only a fast walk, and even then she felt cramps in her thighs and pulling in her groin. So she held her belly with one hand and kept a tight hold on Gabriel's hand with the other. As they hit the trail, she wished she'd thought to find a flashlight, but they couldn't turn back. She did know this darkened trail eventually led to the road, but it was surrounded by thick trees and bushes, and, even in the twilight, it was dark and almost impossible to make her way through. But she was determined, and she poked her way through with Gabriel, who started whining again.

"It's okay, honey. We're almost there." Then they were through, and she could see the pavement of the dark highway. She pulled Gabriel as the pain in her back pinched again, and they started walking.

CHAPTER
Eighteen

"I really appreciate you stopping." Laura shivered in the front seat of a red pickup truck. An older, balding man who smelled as if he'd been around animals all day and had greasy hands drove. Gabriel was in between them and was leaning against Laura, shivering, both of them cold and damp from the rain that had started shortly after they hit the highway. She had been glad when the man stopped, as Gabriel was crying and she didn't think she could take one more step.

"So whereabouts was your car that broke down? Don't remember passing anything on the highway."

"Oh, I pulled off the road when it started sputtering. I know there were a lot of bushes around."

The man grunted and kind of hunched over his steering wheel some more. "A woman in your condition with a little one shouldn't be on the side of the road hitchhiking this time of night."

Laura saw the big sign that was just before the dirt driveway to Diana and Jed's. "Stop right here. There it is."

The man braked and pulled to the side of the road. "This where your brother lives?" he asked.

"Yeah, right down there." Laura gestured and smiled, but she couldn't look the old guy in the eye, with all the lying she'd been doing that night. The man pressed the gas, and Laura glanced up. "What are you doing? You can just let us out here."

"No can do, honey. I knew you were running from something, but Jed Friessen is a good man, a good friend. I can't rightly let no sister of his, as pregnant as you, off on the side of the road in the dark." The man drove down the long dirt driveway and pulled up in front of Jed's darkened house. The engine of the old truck rattled and was enough to wake anyone, so it was no surprise at all when the lights popped on and the front door opened. The old guy turned to Laura. "Whatever trouble you're in, honey, Jed will help you."

Laura unbuckled her seatbelt and leaned over to unfasten Gabriel's, as he'd fallen asleep against her. "Come on, Gabby, open your eyes. We're at Jed and Diana's. Come on." Laura opened her door and slid out, and Gabriel scooted out after her. When she glanced back at the old, grizzled guy who smelled horrible, what she saw was an angel. "Thank you."

He nodded, and she shut the door as Jed stepped out of the house, barefoot in jeans.

"Laura, what are you doing here?" he said.

She started crying, and so did Gabriel.

Nineteen

"Laura, start at the beginning." Diana was wearing a bulky, pink housecoat that barely covered her large, pregnant belly, and she was about to deliver any day.

Jed stepped out of the kitchen with a mug of hot water. "Laura, here, drink this." He handed another to Diana and stood behind her, resting his hands on her shoulders.

Laura sipped on the water. She knew her face was a mess, but she hadn't been able to stop crying since Jed grabbed her and Gabriel and brought them into the house. Diana had hurried from the bedroom, her hair all mussed, pulling a robe over her long night gown. Her expression, from what Laura remembered, had been frantic as she slid her arm around her. Jed had lifted Gabriel and taken him down the hall to their bedroom.

"It was all a game to take my babies. Andy planned it all. As soon as I had them, he was going to take them from me. How could he pretend to care about me, touch me like he did? Gabriel loves him. He was with him every day, tucking him in. Gabriel worships him, and we mean nothing to him. I'm so stupid. How could I have trusted him again?"

"Laura, I need you to back up, because none of this makes any sense. Are you telling me you snuck out with Gabriel and hitchhiked here in your condition?" Jed gestured toward the door and then rested both hands on the chair where Diana was sitting. "So Andy has no idea you left?" Jed's tone was filled with concern, and he shook his head. She wasn't sure whether he was annoyed with her, tired, frustrated, or maybe all three.

"No. I was scared of what would happen. It was the first time I felt like a prisoner, as if someone had control of me. He could have called that bitch of a doctor. She could have given me something and taken my babies now, just like I overheard." She choked again on a sob. "I didn't know where else to go."

"Laura, you were right to come here. Let's just get that straight. Is Gabriel sleeping, Jed?" Diana gazed up at her husband, and they exchanged a look that spouses do when they are so connected to each other.

"He's asleep in our bed." Jed sighed. "Laura, what exactly did you overhear?"

"Everything was going so well. I really thought Andy cared for me. The doctor was supposed to come after lunch, but when I went downstairs, I heard her—the doctor, I mean—and she was talking to Caroline. Caroline asked if it was safe now for me to have my babies, and then the doctor asked her if she had everything taken care of and ready for them. I heard Caroline say that she'd hired a nanny and the nursery was all ready for the babies. Then she said that Andy would finally be rid of me. It was Caroline who said Andy had been pretending with me and that he took after his father that way, and she didn't know how he could stand to be around me. To her, I'm just trash. I always knew Caroline didn't like me, but then I heard the doctor say she'd do a C-section on me and I wouldn't see my babies. They were planning this. I'd wake up and my babies would be gone." She gasped and covered her mouth. She was going to wake Danny and Gabriel if she kept talking, as she couldn't keep the panic out of her voice.

Jed and Diana exchanged a look again. There was an array of emotions that crossed Diana's face. Jed rested his hand on her shoulder and squeezed, and Diana's hand was trembling when she reached up and slid her hand into his.

"Laura, I'm really confused. I know Andy can be a real bastard, and he's done some things I'd like to knock his teeth out for. You heard this doctor and Caroline talking—was Andy there, too?" Jed asked.

"No, I don't think so. I didn't hear him with them. When I heard Caroline and the doctor go into the dining room, I went back upstairs, and I tried to do it quietly so they wouldn't know I was there. I was scared, and then I started opening doors to all the rooms upstairs. In the other wing, there was a nursery all put together, with cradles and two cribs and a rocker, clothes, diapers, and baby furniture...and it was all ready for my babies. I saw it. I didn't know what to do, and when I was hurrying back to our room, Andy came up the stairs with the doctor. He pretended to care about me, and he knew something was wrong even though I tried to hide it. And...I couldn't. I never could lie. He knows, or he has to suspect that I know."

Jed stepped back and wiped his hand roughly over his face. He strode down the hall, and Diana watched her husband return a few seconds later, buttoning a plaid shirt, tucking it into his jeans, then shoving his feet into his cowboy boots. When he lifted his lined jean jacket from the hook, Diana said, "Jed, where are you going this time of night?"

He strode straight to his wife and leaned down, touching her lips with his and cupping her face with his one hand. It was such a possessive thing to do that Laura was in awe watching them, as her entire security and sense of self crumbled all around her. Why couldn't Andy have looked at her that way, loved her that way? It hurt to watch when she longed to have that for herself.

"I'm going to pay my cousin a visit."

Laura jerked her gaze up at Jed and felt panic sizzle the back of her neck. "Jed, no. Please don't tell him I'm here. Please don't talk to him. He's got money and power, and he can make me disappear." She was on her feet, her hands fisted at her side.

Jed reached for her, taking both of her arms, and held her much like he would a child he was about to give a talking to. "You're safe here. No one is coming in and taking you. And his money, power, and crap means nothing here. You ought to know that, Laura. But he is my cousin, and if he did do this and is part of something this criminal and despicable, I will take him down. No one's taking your babies from you." Jed sat her back down on the sofa. "Diana, keep her inside. I don't know how long I'll be."

Diana waddled over to the kitchen and yanked a cell phone from the charger. "Take this and call me. Keep it on so I can get a hold of you."

Jed didn't hesitate and shoved the cell phone in his jacket pocket. "I won't be long." He grabbed his cowboy hat, stuck it on his head over his sleep-tousled, short, brown hair, and jingled the truck keys as he yanked the door open. "Lock this behind me. Don't let anyone in."

Diana strode to the door as Laura listened to a truck start up. Diana locked the door and peeked through the curtains. "Laura, Jed is right. I'm hoping what you heard was all a misunderstanding, but I also know that Caroline is a dangerous snake. She comes from old money; a family that lives and breathes corruption, destroying anyone who gets in her way. But why would she want your babies? I can't figure that one out. Nevertheless, you're safe here. My husband will not allow this to happen, Laura." Diana stepped away from the curtains and sat beside Laura on the sofa.

"Thank you, Diana. I'm so sorry. I just didn't know what to do."

Diana picked Laura's hand up. She stared at the diamond-encrusted band and frowned. "Is that new?"

"Yes, it is. Andy bought it for me. I know it cost a fortune. I don't know why he did it."

"Hmm." Diana patted her hand.

"What does that mean?" Laura asked.

"It means that we wait for Jed. We wait for my husband to talk to your husband. So get comfortable, honey; we're in for a long night."

Twenty

"Where the hell is she?" Andy barked at Jules, who was in her robe, her hair in curlers.

He'd woken the entire household while looking for Laura, and he still couldn't believe she was gone. Walking into their room to get ready for bed and finding the bed empty, the covers thrown back in a crumpled heap, he'd checked the bathroom. When he couldn't find her, he wondered if maybe she was looking for him, but when he spotted Gabriel's open door and peeked in, it had taken him a second to realize the bed was empty. He had flicked on the bedroom light, and, sure enough, he was gone.

Maybe Gabriel had woken Laura. Maybe he was thirsty. Andy had jogged down the stairs and gone into a darkened kitchen, flicking on the light. There wasn't even a glass on the counter or in the sink of the spotless kitchen.

He had searched his library, the sunroom, the entire downstairs, and then he went back to their bedroom. The open closet door beckoned, and when he stepped in and looked around, he had spotted the empty shelf where the running shoes he'd bought her had been. A price tag lay on the floor, and as he bent over and picked up the white ticket, he felt sucker punched. A sense of betrayal blew through him. He knew she had been upset all day, as if she couldn't stand his touch or to be around him. He'd ignored his instincts, which had been sending alarm bells off inside of him, screaming that there was a problem. Instead, he had listened to the doctor, who said women this far in pregnancy often became irritable and didn't want to be touched. Yeah, bullshit. He'd known something wasn't right. Hell, it had only been hours since he'd taken her on the bed, a slow ride so full of passion that he couldn't get enough of her. He had felt the sparks he was shooting off inside of her.

"Sir, we've looked everywhere. She's not here, but Thomas found the door by your mother's wing unlocked."

The doorbell chimed. Andy started back down the stairs. It was after midnight, so dread deepened and squeezed his heart with each step. No one in their right mind was out knocking on doors this time of night. He yanked the door open and stared into the hardened face of his cousin.

"You missing someone, coz?" Jed snapped. He pushed his way inside, bumping Andy as he stepped in.

Andy shut the door, and when the stairs creaked behind him, he spun around, his gaze landing on Jules, who hovered halfway down the stairs. "That's all for tonight Jules."

She gave a curt nod and climbed down the stairs, heading to where her small suite was at the rear of the house.

"Where is my wife, Jed?" Andy snapped.

"She showed up damn near falling apart on my doorstep with Gabriel, both of them wet and cold and crying. She told quite the tale, as well, of how you're plotting to take her babies from her with some lady doctor." Jed shoved his hands on his hips, and Andy knew from the look in his cousin's eyes that Jed wouldn't hesitate to punch him in the face.

"What the hell? That is absolutely insane." Andy stalked into his library to grab his keys from the desk, shoving them in his pocket.

"You ain't going out there, Andy; not until I find out what the hell's going on. I gave Laura my word that she'd be safe, and I mean that. She will. Now I want to know why your wife is so freaked out." Jed was right behind him, lifting the cowboy hat from his head and dumping it on Andy's desk. "Sit down, coz."

"I'm not sitting down. I want to talk some sense into my wife. Where in the hell would she come up with a ridiculous accusation like that? I thought we were past this." Andy tried to go around Jed, because, right now, he wanted nothing more than to put his hands on Laura and shake her senseless, but Jed put his hand on Andy's shoulder and stopped him.

"Whoa there, Andy. I guess you're not hearing me. You're not going out there now. She's a mess, and she's terrified of you. My wife is about ready to deliver any day, so you're not turning my house upside down."

Andy held up both his hands in surrender. "Where would she get the idea I'd take the babies from her? What kind of monster does she think I am? I wouldn't do that. I just got her and Gabriel back. I..." He had to stop himself, because he had almost said he loved her.

"Apparently, she overheard your mother and that doctor planning a C-section for her and saying they would take the babies away before she could see them. Your mother told this doctor woman that everything's been taken care of. A nanny's been hired, and the nursery is ready and waiting for the babies. She said you were anxious to be rid of Laura and that all you've been doing is pretending with her, that apparently you take after Todd that way." Jed then stared at Andy, watching him and waiting for his response.

Andy couldn't find his voice. Everything he'd worked for with Laura had disintegrated like fine sand through his fingers. He sat on the edge of his desk and took a deep breath. He didn't know what to make of this tale Jed was telling. Laura couldn't have heard right.

"We have yet to start a nursery for the babies. I never thought that far ahead. I was worried about Laura. This makes no sense; she couldn't have heard that." He gestured with his hands sharply as he paced. "What the hell would my mother want with the babies? God, I was just an afterthought for her, an annoyance and an obligation to carry on the name. She had to have heard wrong. Doctor Richardson is one of the best OBs around. What's in it for her? This makes no sense."

"Andy, apparently Laura found the nursery in this house. She said it's in your mother's wing."

Andy snapped his head up and felt a surge of fire rocketing him off that desk. He took the stairs two at a time, and Jed was right behind him. Andy started opening doors at the end of the hall, banging them open, flicking on lights. He froze in the third room, his hand still hovering on the light switch, as he stared at the suite, decorated in white and lavender with a hint of gold on the trim. It was a fully furnished nursery with two of everything, as if waiting for his babies.

"Oh my God." It was all he could say as he stepped in the room, jamming his fingers in his hair and yanking. He turned in a circle and stared at Jed, who was frowning and eyeing the entire room. "Jed, I swear to God I didn't know this was here. I'd never do this to Laura."

Jed was watching him in a hard, mysterious way. Andy didn't know what he was thinking. Then he flicked his gaze away and nodded.

"Yeah, well, you can be an unscrupulous bastard, Andy, but I didn't think this had you written on it." Jed faced Andy again. "You know Laura's not going to come back here."

"I know. But I need to see her."

Jed nodded and started out the door. "Well, it might help if you tell her how you really feel about her, too."

"I'm not letting her go, Jed."

Jed started walking. "Yeah, well, I was hoping you would say that. Do you want to ride with me?"

Andy hurried down the stairs, side by side with Jed. "I'll follow you. Just do me a favor, Jed." He stopped at the bottom of the stairs, watching Jed study him in that inflexible way of his. "When you call Diana, don't tell her I'm coming for Laura. You and I both know she'll start running again."

"You right behind me?"

Andy grabbed his leather coat from the closet. "Let's go."

He followed his cousin out the door, but what he didn't see was Caroline, watching from the second floor railing, tapping her long, manicured nails on the wood rail.

Twenty~One

Andy followed Jed's truck, keeping the red taillights as his guide all the way out to his ranch. It wasn't so much that he didn't know the way, because he could do this drive in his sleep. It was that he'd felt his entire world and everything he believed crumble around him. The entire drive, he waged a battle with his emotions, from the horror he felt at the thought of Laura having been on the side of the highway, drenched from the rain at night with Gabriel, to the fury he felt towards her for having run away. They could have been killed, since people couldn't see squat as the rain came down on the black pavement, with no moon or lights anywhere.

Who had picked them up on the side of the road? He forgot to ask Jed that part. The fact that she had run and didn't trust him enough to ask him, to just know he wouldn't do something that horrible, cut into his heart and burned as if someone were pouring acid over an open wound. Couldn't she see how much she meant to him?

By the time he had pulled in front of Jed's house, beside his truck, he'd tossed every conceivable dark thing that could have happened to Laura and Gabriel through his mind, and he wanted to punch something. He still couldn't get past his need to put his hands on his wife and shake her senseless. What the hell were they doing with all this running? He loved Gabriel, and that boy needed him. He knew deep down that Laura did, too, but this had now become a matter of trust.

Jed waited for him to walk around the front of his truck, and even in the pitch black of night, the little house looked so warm and welcoming that Andy was glad that Laura had come here.

———

SHE FELT the touch on her shoulder, the strong hand. For a moment, as she slowly woke and opened her eyes, she felt safe, until she blinked a couple times and her awareness returned. She remembered what she'd run from and was stung by the betrayal. She could smell him, and he still had that scent that reeled her to him. She realized she'd become a yo-yo, back and forth, between loving him and having her guts ripped and shredded, crying over him night after night. She needed to hate him, she had to, and as he slid his arm under her and helped her sit up on the sofa where she'd lain down and fallen asleep, her heart did a flip-flop right before she felt everything beneath her crumble when she glimpsed a shimmer of tears in those mesmerizing blue eyes.

"You scared the life out of me. What the hell, Laura...?" She could see the tremble in his jaw as he clamped it tight. "Why would you believe I could do something that despicable?"

His hands were on her, holding her shoulders, holding

her. She glimpsed Diana and Jed hovering in the background, Jed holding Diana in his arms.

"I heard them, Andy. Are you telling me you didn't know? How am I supposed to believe that, Andy, after what I heard?" Her voice sounded rough.

"It's about trust, Laura. I thought we'd gotten there. Answer this for me: Did you hear my voice? Because you wouldn't have. My God, you think I could pretend when I had you under me, making love to you, that you meant something you don't? You must believe I'm the worst kind of monster and one hell of an actor if you think I could pull that off." He spat out the words, and his hands gripped her shoulders a little harder than usual. She could feel the battle he waged inside himself. He probably wanted to shake her until her teeth rattled.

"Andy, I felt sucker punched, and I..." She bit her tongue because she couldn't tell him how she felt about him. She couldn't tell him she loved him. "How I feel about you and us, I have never been so scared in my life. I felt trapped, imprisoned. Someone had power over me. They could take my babies and discard me as if I were nothing. And I heard your mother...."

"My mother has no say in my life, in our life, in our babies' lives," Andy barked out.

Laura watched the odd expression exchanged between Diana and Jed, and she had a sick feeling that what she believed wasn't so black and white.

"Are you telling me that you didn't know anything about Doctor Richardson's plans for a C-section and to take my babies? What about the nursery that I found in the house? That is not a coincidence, Andy—not at all." She was having a hard time talking, as her throat had thickened. What had she done? She felt sick all of sudden at sneaking out the way she did, without even leaving a note for Andy. What must he have thought?

She couldn't stop the tremble in her face as she felt herself falling apart again. The tears, there was no stopping them. She looked at the one man she truly loved, the first man who'd stolen her heart, and there was no hope she'd ever get it back. He had the power to crush her, to love her and destroy her. As she felt the sofa sink beside her and Andy's thigh press against hers, he slid his arm around her and pulled her into his embrace. She couldn't speak, but she did hold on to his jacket and bury her face into him, breathing him in, his earthy fragrance that her body craved, just like the nutrients she needed to nurture her babies.

"Laura, Andy didn't know anything about this," Jed said, speaking up.

She nodded and just let Andy hold her. She couldn't speak, because she was ashamed that she'd leaped on that wagon, thinking he was the evildoer instead of trusting and talking to him. Hindsight was a powerful tool to have. Hadn't she and Andy just traveled this road? They were still dirty and dusty, with the treads burned into them.

"I'm so sorry." She couldn't stop crying.

"Well, why the hell didn't you ask me? Why couldn't you trust me? You should have come to me as soon as you heard what you did and told me, Laura."

If she wasn't pregnant, she was pretty sure he would have pulled away, because she could feel his tightly coiled anger all wrapped up with confusion and frustration. Could she blame him? She wanted to kick herself and didn't know what to say to make it up to him.

"I can't do this with you running away. You either want to be my wife, Laura, or you don't."

She nodded. She was too choked up to get the words

out, as her throat had long since closed up. Then, ever so slowly, she slid her hand down his arm to his wrist, and she rested her hand on his thigh as if she had every right, and he flinched. She sat up, and his arm was still looped around her, and she stared at him through a haze. She swiped at her eyes roughly, feeling the sting, then at her nose with her sleeve.

"I do." She nodded again when she choked.

"Laura, I need to know this time whether you're all in, because when I opened that door to our bedroom and saw the empty bed, and then Gabriel's, too, I searched the entire house, and you have no idea the dark places my head went. Then I find out that you had snuck out the back door like some thief in the night and hitchhiked along a dark highway, in the condition you're in, with Gabriel, who had to be terrified. You could have been killed or hurt, you and Gabriel. I can't do this anymore with you."

"I love you, Andy, and I'm sorry, but when I heard Doctor Richardson say she'd do a C-section on me and take my babies so that I couldn't see them, and then your mother said you were pretending with me and you couldn't wait to be rid of me; I didn't want to believe it, but then I saw that nursery. You don't know what that did to me. I wanted to hate you, but I still couldn't, because I gave you my heart long ago and I never got it back. I didn't want to tell you because you have the power to rip my heart to shreds, but you've never told me once how you feel about me."

He held her face in his one hand as if making her look at him, and what she saw tore her heart open a little more. "Don't you know how I feel? My God, Laura, I am not that good of an actor. Yes, I've always cared for you, and when you walked out the first time, I felt like crap because I didn't treat you as I should have. But this time, when I got you back, Laura, we... Couldn't you tell how I felt about you?"

"I need to hear it, Andy. I need you to tell me how you feel, because I don't want to have to guess and wonder whether it's just my imagination. You made me feel like an obligation, and you know you did. Then, this last time, I knew you cared, but I couldn't help wondering if it was just because of the babies."

He shut his eyes and glanced away for a second, but he didn't let go of her face, as if he was hanging on to her.

She slid her hand over his. "Please, Andy."

"Yeah, well, baby, you had me long ago. I didn't want to admit it. You can't keep running away, Laura. I need you to promise me you won't run again, because I love you. When you do this—take off, I feel as if you've scraped away all that's good between us and thrown it back in my face. And Gabriel, I love him as if he's mine. You can't just take him anymore; you can't let him build a relationship with me and rip that away from him—and from me. You're not being fair, Laura."

No one said anything. Laura watched him. His expression was a mirror of what she'd felt, somewhere between love and frustration and hurt. She felt everything that she knew to be a real shift, as if the room had tilted and the only thing she could do was reach out to Andy as he dropped his hand from her face and fisted it as if he had to fight to keep from touching her.

She ran her hand over his face and the scratchy dark whiskers. She ran her thumb over his lips and realized he was so tired. He'd been handling everything, and how must he have felt to hear what his mother had done?

"All I can say, Andy, is that I'm sorry. I didn't want to believe it, but I was scared. I didn't know, and I wish I could go back and talk to you, but I can't. I won't run again, but I'm not going back to that house, Andy. I will not live under the same roof as your mother. I don't want her in my life, but I want you."

"Andy, you need to find out about this doctor lady, too." Jed was holding Diana in his arms, watching Laura and Andy.

"Jed's right, Andy. If what Laura heard this doctor say to Caroline, doing a C-section, taking her babies from her, well, I'd say this is grounds to have this doctor's medical license revoked. Maybe talk to the sheriff. Mention it, but keep in mind it could come down to Laura's words against a prominent doctor and your mother, especially since there were no witnesses," Diana said, her voice filled with emotion. "Andy, for what it's worth, that's every woman's worst nightmare, that someone will take her baby, especially someone she should feel safe with."

"Look, we're all tired," Jed said. "It's been a long night, and the kids are going to be up soon. Andy, why don't you and Laura stay up in the loft above the barn? Everything's still there for you." Jed gestured to the door. "Andy, we'll talk in the morning about this doctor of yours."

Andy stood up and pulled Laura up with him. Laura felt his arm tighten around her.

"I'll grab Gabriel take him with us," he said.

Andy started down the hall when Diana said, "No, leave him. Jed will move him into Danny's room. You two, go get some sleep. I know I'm about ready to fall over."

Laura didn't know what to say. Her head was so thick she couldn't think clearly. She wanted to sleep now for a week, because she had Andy and she wanted to lean into him and just let everything go. As soon as he stepped beside her, she took his hand.

"Thank you, Jed, Diana, for everything. I don't know what to say," she said.

"Just get some sleep, Laura. Your husband and I will deal with this in the morning."

Laura didn't miss the sharp look shared between both men and then Diana, who glanced at the ceiling and shook her head as if she'd been down that road one too many times with a man who was going to handle something whether she wanted him to or not.

"Jed" was all Andy said as he ushered Laura out the door into the dark.

"You want a flashlight?" Jed called after them.

Andy had his arm around Laura, leading to the darkened barn. "No."

"I can't see anything, Andy." Laura gripped his wrist, and when she stumbled, all Andy did was scoop her up in his arms. "Andy, I'm too heavy," she said as she slid her arms around his neck and rested her head against his shoulder. She took a deep breath of the rich leather of his coat. It was so him, all his scent.

"The day I can't carry you is the day you can put me out in the field. I won't be of any use to you." Andy pulled her closer, his arm under her knees, the other around her back, carrying her with no effort as he yanked open the sliding barn door. He juggled Laura and strode in the dark barn to the door that led up to the loft, and he flicked on the lights and carried Laura up the stairs, setting her on the bed.

"It's cold up here." Laura shivered.

Andy helped Laura up and slid her sweater down her arms. "Get undressed and in bed. You'll warm up under the covers. I'm going to lock up."

Laura grabbed his arm. "I don't want you to go. Please don't leave me."

He slid both hands over her cheeks, holding her face up to him. "I'm not leaving you. I'm just going to shut the barn door so critters aren't wandering in the barn, and locking our door so that no one can get in. I'll be right back."

The floor creaked under the weight of Andy's feet as he pounded down the stairs. She listened as the barn door squeaked closed, and then the door at the bottom of the stairs. He turned the deadbolt and then climbed back up, and Laura just stood there watching.

"Get undressed and in bed. Come on, you're shivering."

Andy slid his hands under her shirt and lifted it over her head so that Laura stood in just her bra and pants. He sat her on the bed, and she couldn't shake the feeling of being treasured. He lifted her foot and removed first one shoe then the other, then helped her stand again and unclasped her bra, tossing it onto the floor as he slid his hands over her large breasts, now a C cup. Andy rubbed his palms over her nipples, and she leaned her head back and gasped. He slid his hand around her back and held her so she didn't fall, and he lowered his head to her neck, breathing her in as she slid her arms around his neck and held him.

Andy kissed her neck and then her cheek, then brushed her lips with his, and she pressed her tongue to his, needing to taste him, be part of him. He pulled the tie holding up her cotton pants and then shoved his hands in the waistband, pushing them down with her underwear until they pooled at her feet. "Step out." He tore his lips away and then reached behind her, pulling the covers back. "Get in."

"I want you in bed with me." She pulled on his arm as he helped her under the covers, the chill of the icy sheets hitting her bare skin made her teeth start to chatter.

"Oh, I plan on doing just that." He pulled the quilt up to her chin and then tossed his leather coat on the kitchen chair, unbuttoning his shirt, toeing his boots off and unbuckling his belt without taking his eyes off her.

With the warmth in his eyes and what she knew was coming with him, with his touch, his caress, she began to warm in anticipation. Even the doubt and uncertainty that had lingered in her heart, for the first time in forever, was gone.

Laura leaned back against Andy, loving the sense of being his, feeling every part of him, so very male and warm and strong, pressing into her. It was as if a piece of her very own heaven had been cut out and handed to her on her very own platter, and there was only here and now, no tomorrow and no yesterday. He had a way of making her feel safe now that she had dropped all of the walls she'd kept nailing up around her, and if Dr. Richardson or Caroline or anyone tried to break through that door right now, she knew without a shadow of a doubt that they wouldn't get past her husband.

He kissed her shoulder and then slid his hand over her large belly, over his babies, and she linked her fingers with his, loving the feel of his large hand.

"I love you," she whispered, breathing in the cool air.

"Hmm," he murmured, nuzzling her ear. "I didn't hurt you, did I?"

"No, you feel so good. I can still feel you."

Andy slid his hand over her hip. "You need to get some sleep."

Laura turned her head toward him. "What about the doctor and what she said she was going to do? I don't want her anywhere around me or delivering the babies."

Andy rose up on his elbow so he could easily look down into her eyes. "Don't you worry about Doctor Richardson. I'll deal with her. I want you to relax. You need to let me handle this."

"But, Andy, what are you going to do? I mean, I heard Jed, what he said...."

"Laura, go to sleep. There is nothing for you to worry about. This is my responsibility. I'll handle it." He cut her off, and his expression appeared to darken, but it wasn't for her. He leaned down and kissed her, and for the first time, she didn't feel the need to wonder and worry. She really believed that he would handle it.

"You make me feel so safe, Andy." She yawned because letting go and being able to lean on Andy had her so relaxed that she thought maybe she could sleep for a week. So she snuggled into his arms, one hand resting on his very sexy hip, the other linked with his, feeling as if she was nestled in a very protective cocoon. She felt the tension melt from every muscle, every limb, until she was so relaxed that she felt herself floating to a place of absolute peace.

She didn't know what woke her, she lay there in that place, not really awake, listening to Andy's heavy breathing behind her where she was still pressed against him. She first became aware of the cramping down her thighs, and it brought her instantly alert. She waited for it to pass as it slowly grew stronger, as if someone had pulled the belt tighter around her and then let it go. She breathed out and blinked in the darkness. How long had she been asleep? She didn't know, but as the cramping passed, she became aware of an ache pinching her lower back. It had been there last night and must have come from all the running she'd done, dragging Gabriel down a darkened path. She had pushed herself too hard—of course she did. After all, she'd been on bed rest, and Andy had all but waited on her hand and foot. Her body wasn't used to this. She needed to move, as the cramping in her back was getting worse, and she hated moving because Andy was so tired and he was such a light sleeper that she didn't want to wake him. She didn't want to move out of the comfort of his arms.

"What's wrong?" Andy muttered in a deep, groggy voice.

"I didn't want to wake you. It's just that my back hurts," Laura said. Then she felt the cramping again down her thighs and lower belly. "Ohh," she groaned as she pulled her knees up and blew out as the tightening seemed to go on longer, stealing her breath.

Andy was now sitting up and leaning over her, rubbing her arm. "Are you having contractions, Laura?" He sounded wide awake now.

It took Laura a minute before she could answer. "I don't know. My back was hurting. I just thought I did too much last night."

"I'm going to call the doctor." Andy started to get out of bed.

"No, don't call that doctor. I don't want her anywhere near me and the babies. She's going to hurt me, take our babies." Laura started to cry, and Andy slid his hand under her shoulder and lifted her as she struggled to sit up. He held her against his warm chest.

"Shh, don't cry. I'm not calling Doctor Richardson. I'm going to take you to the hospital."

"No, I don't want to go to the hospital. Andy, please."

"Laura, it's too early for you to have the babies. I'm going to wake Jed, get the name of Diana's doctor." Andy slid out of bed and had his jeans on in a second. He sat beside her on the bed and pulled on his boots. "Look, I want to talk to someone to make sure that you and the babies are okay. I promise I'm not going to let anything happen. You've got to trust me, Laura."

"Andy, I do trust you. I'm just scared."

He touched her face with both hands, and she grabbed both his wrists, holding on to him because she didn't want him to go. Andy leaned in and kissed her lightly.

"I'm not going to let anything happen to you. No one is taking our babies."

She watched him, and something inside the blue-gray of his eyes had her heart doing a flip-flop. That wolf, predator, and protector was all around her. *My God* was all she could think as she swallowed and then finally nodded, hypnotized. She felt the sync of his flow, and she wasn't on the outside looking in. It was powerful and beyond words, and it was all she had ever wanted. So absolutely, yes, she trusted him with her life, her babies' lives.

"I'll be right back." He grabbed his coat off of the chair and pulled it on as he hurried down the steps, and Laura listened as she felt the tightening low in her pelvis, across the front and down her thighs, and she rocked on the bed and groaned from the ache. It was stronger, longer, and it was just passing when she heard footsteps, Andy running up the steps and another behind him. She pulled the blanket up over her breasts, as she sat naked under the covers.

"You have another contraction?" Andy said. He was behind her on the bed. Jed was standing by the stairs, and she felt so exposed. Andy must have known, as he reached for his shirt on the chair and helped her put it on, buttoning up the front. "The bed's wet," Andy said as he pulled back the covers.

"I think my water broke." Laura could feel it trickling out of her. "Can I have a towel? The mattress is soaked under me."

"Diana's calling her doctor, Laura, but it sounds like you two need to go to the hospital now." Jed was standing over them.

"Jed's right, Laura. We need to go now. I'll help you get dressed." Andy was off the bed, reaching for the clothes tossed on the floor.

"No, I don't want to go, Andy. I want to have the babies here."

Both men gave her a look as if she'd just lost her mind.

"You're thirty-three weeks. It's too early; there could be complications, and you're having twins. We are not staying here. You are having these babies in the hospital, where there are doctors and nurses who know what to do if something goes wrong, where there is medical equipment."

Jed opened his mouth as if trying to figure out what to say. Andy was now pacing beside the bed, the wolf she'd come to know as part of who he was wound so tightly that she wondered for a moment whether he wouldn't reach down and scoop her up. She could also see that he was holding himself back from leaping in, taking her, dumping her in his truck, and driving fast and furious to the hospital.

He pressed his fingertips to his eyes and hovered above her. "Laura, you are going to the hospital...."

She didn't hear what else he said, because another contraction squeezed, shooting pain like shards of glass jabbing into her thighs. It was the worst yet, and she rocked on the bed and moaned. "Oh, Andy..."

The bed squeaked, and the mattress dipped beside her. His hand was pressed against her lower back, rubbing, his other across her front so she could lean into him.

"Andy, it hurts. I don't remember it being so hard."

"That's pretty close together, Laura," Jed said. The floor creaked as he stepped closer. "Andy, you need to talk your wife into going to the hospital, or you should just take her."

"No, I don't want to go. Please, Jed, if I'm in the hospital, that doctor could sneak in and take my babies, our babies, Andy. If they planned this, how easy would it be for them to do it, give me a shot, put me out? I know it sounds paranoid. I'm scared, and it's nothing to do with me not trusting you, Andy, because I do. I just don't trust what they'd do."

Laura rode out another wave of contractions and leaned against Andy, fisting his leather coat, squeezing it. His chin rested on top of her head. She heard him say something to Jed and listened to Jed's footsteps going down the stairs, but that was all that registered in her brain. She was simply here with Andy, thinking the pain, becoming a part of it.

"Laura, you're fighting it. Breathe, come on, take a deep breath and let it out—and again."

She listened to his voice and did what he said, and it helped. She wanted to sag into him when it passed, because she was so tired.

She knew the sound of Jed's heavy footsteps as he hurried back up. The hardwood stairs and the open beam brought an echo every time someone came up or even walked across the floor. Laura welcomed the sound because she loved it here; it was safe and a haven, and to her, it was a comfort.

"Diana just spoke with her doctor. She wants to know how close together they are. She said she'll meet you at the hospital."

"Still no cell service out here, right?" Andy was on his

feet, reaching into his coat pocket for his cell phone and holding it up. "Shit, nothing. Jesus, Jed, of all times for you to live out in the middle of nowhere."

"Andy..." Laura called out to him and let out a loud groan. The pain was tearing at her thighs and in her back, and she thought she'd go out of her mind. He was beside her again, and she leaned on him as he rubbed her back and talked her through it. Then it passed.

"That's pretty close together. Two minutes, Jed. Call your doctor back. Tell her we'll meet her at the hospital. I'm taking Laura now."

Jed took off down the stairs again.

Laura didn't want to go, but she was also scared now because she didn't think she could handle this. Andy grabbed her pants on the floor and held them so she could step into them. "Laura, come on, put your legs in."

She slid her legs over the side of the bed, pulling back the damp covers. She could still feel the amniotic fluid running out of her. "Andy, my pants are going to be soaked. It's going to look like I peed myself." She put her feet in, and Andy lifted her up and slid them over her hips.

"I don't care. I'm getting you to the hospital if I have to wrap you in a blanket and carry you naked."

"Andy," Jed shouted up, "Diana's on the phone inside with her doctor. She's on her way, but she has to drive past us. She said Laura's contractions sound too close together. She'll be here first if you want to wait. She also said to call an ambulance. Don't drive, or you may be delivering on the side of the road."

"Andy, there's another one coming."

Andy had her lean against the bed rail, his hand pressed into her back. "Come on, breathe through it. You know this. We learned all of this. Let it go; focus on your breathing." His voice and the strength in it brought her through and over the peak of the pain, his hand rubbing her lower back as if he knew instinctively where the pressure and burning ache came from.

"Andy, oh my God, it hurts."

"I know it does," Andy said. His voice was her anchor, and he spoke deeply and softly. She held on to that, just like his arm, which snaked around her front, holding her shoulders. She reached for his forearm and held tight. She felt weak and tired when it passed, but she'd only just started.

Footsteps pounded up the stairs again. "Diana's calling an ambulance. Her doctor's here, Doctor Caldwell."

Laura was still holding the bedframe when a dark, mocha-skinned doctor with light brown eyes and dark hair pulled tight in a ponytail set a bag on the table.

"Hi, you must be Laura. When was your last contraction, honey?"

"She just had it," Andy said. "I'm her husband, Andy. Did Diana and Jed tell you why she called?"

"Quite a tale I was told. Don't know if I believe it, but let's get your wife settled and looked after. Laura, I want you back on the bed so I can check you and see how far you've progressed."

Andy helped Laura back on the bed.

"Let's get your pants off, too." The doctor was short and a little on the chunky side. She had full, dark lips and a no-bullshit attitude that made Laura want to trust her. "Jed, I'm going to need some towels here, too. Laura, it looks like you're leaking some amniotic fluid."

"My water broke. The bed is wet," Laura said.

Andy slid off her pants. "Come on, Laura. Lift your butt."

The doctor pulled a rubber glove from her bag and slipped it on. "If you feel a contraction, you need to tell me." She slipped her fingers inside and stared up at Andy. Jed was just outside the bathroom. The doctor shook her head. "Jed, see if the paramedics are here. Laura, you're ten centimeters, honey, fully dilated. I'm going to need you to start pushing."

"Well, how can that be? My labor started not long ago."

"Any back pain?" she asked and reached for the towels Jed held out to her.

"Yeah, last night or tonight when I left, my back was killing me all the way here. That was around nine. I don't even know what time it is!" Laura cried.

"It's four in the morning, way too early for anyone in their right mind to be up. Jed, also, when you're down there to get the paramedics, tell them I need a clamp and mask. They'll know. Just tell them Mom's in active labor, twins early at..." She hesitated and looked to Andy just as Laura felt another contraction pull her in. The muscles tightened her back, her thighs, across her belly and went on and on.

"She's thirty-three weeks," Andy said as he rested his hand on Laura's bare hip.

"Oh, I need to push!" she screamed, grabbing the side of the mattress and squeezing it.

"Okay, Laura, how do you want to deliver? On your side, your back?" the doctor asked, but Laura couldn't answer. "Andy, get behind your wife. Get her up. Laura, legs apart. Come on. You're going to push when I tell you and push with the contraction."

The doctor slid a towel under her butt, and Andy's shirt was pushed up.

Andy was behind her, and he had her lean against him and took both of her hands in his. He kissed her cheek. "You can do this."

"As soon as the next contraction hits, I want you to start pushing," the doctor said. She rested her hand on Laura's knee, pushing it open wider.

It was so fast, the power of the next contraction, that they were almost on top of each other, so strong she felt as if they were ripping her apart. She screamed as she pushed, and Andy was loud and demanding in her ear, telling her to push, to keep going.

"I can see the head. Stop pushing, Laura."

"Oh, it hurts," she cried out and rolled her head against Andy's shoulder. "Andy, I can't do this. It hurts so much."

"Yes, you can," he said sharply as he held her, his lips against her ear, his warm breath on her cheek. "I'm getting you through this. Just you and me, let's bring this baby in."

"Laura, slow and easy, just a small push. Okay, stop. The head's out."

Laura could hear commotion, voices, people coming up the stairs, two paramedics and Jed, and she didn't care who saw her like this, not at this point. She just wanted her baby out, the pain to stop, for this to be over.

"Laura, okay, push again on the next contraction." Dr. Caldwell was sitting right on the bed, her hands gloved. "Cord's around the neck. Okay, it's off."

Laura didn't really know who the doctor was talking to, but there was a man there now, speaking to her. The last contraction ripped through her, and she pushed and yelled, squeezing Andy's hand hard.

"That's it. The shoulders are out. Stop pushing, Laura. Ah, there we go."

Laura waited but didn't hear anything. "I can't hear my baby," she said.

The doctor said nothing, but her face was harried, and she clamped and cut the umbilical cord. "Mask here now!"

she shouted at the paramedics, who hovered while the doctor used a suction in the baby's mouth and then put a mask over it, squeezing it three, four times. Then the baby cried. "That was way too close." She wrapped the baby in a towel. "Here, Mom. It's a girl."

Laura stared at the angelic tiny face on her naked belly and held her. It was Andy who touched her tiny finger and asked, "What happened?"

"Cord was around the baby's neck. We were lucky. Let's get her to the hospital now. I'm not chancing anything else going wrong. I'm operating blind, and I don't like that." She turned to the paramedics. "Can you bring the stretcher up here?"

"I'll carry my wife down. Jed, take our baby." Andy reached for their tiny daughter, who just fit in his large hand. He watched her for a second and then kissed her forehead before putting her in Jed's arms.

"I've got her. Get your wife down to the ambulance," Jed said.

Andy grabbed the quilt at the foot of the bed and wrapped Laura in it, lifting her and carrying her down. The paramedics had already gone down first and had the back door of the ambulance open. The doctor and Jed followed. Diana was outside by the ambulance now, waiting in her housecoat, and she looked tired, worried, and scared for Laura.

"Laura, we've got Gabriel. Don't you worry," Diana said to her as Andy stepped into the ambulance and laid her on the stretcher.

Jed handed the baby to the doctor. "It's a girl," he said to his wife, and as she peeked at the baby the doctor was holding, her face lit up.

"Oh, she's so beautiful," Diana whispered.

"Laura, how're you doing?" the doctor asked as she

handed the baby to the short, balding paramedic in back with them, who set the baby in the crook of Laura's arm on the gurney.

"I'm sore, but I haven't had another contraction like I did. Is that normal?" Laura gazed into the face of her daughter. She was moving her tiny mouth, and it looked so much like Andy's.

"Having twins, there is nothing normal, but it happens where contractions slow. Let's get going. I want to get an ultrasound on the next one." The doctor climbed in and sat beside Andy on the bench.

The back doors shut, and the ambulance started moving. Andy caressed Laura's cheek, pushing her damp hair back, and the expression on Andy's face, in his touch, was filled with so much love that she thought her heart would burst. When he looked down at his daughter, she knew without a doubt that not one of them would ever be an afterthought.

Twenty-Three

"My leg's wet. I feel wet. I'm not feeling so good," Laura said and then searched out Andy. "Andy, take our baby. Don't let her go."

The doctor had pulled the blanket back, and Andy slipped the baby in his arms. Laura's face paled. The pink cheeks and all the color she'd had moments ago appeared to drain away.

"Okay, she's bleeding. I'm blind, here. She could be delivering the placenta for the first one. I need some light here. Andy, do you remember what Doctor Richardson said about the twins? Are they sharing the same sac? Fraternal twins, identical?" The doctor spoke fast, but there was an edge of urgency to her voice.

"They have their own sac. She said they're not identical. I remember she said fraternal twins. What's going on?" Andy asked sharply as he watched over Laura, who had beads of sweat on her forehead and was lying so quietly, watching him as if she wanted to go to sleep.

"ETA, five minutes to the hospital!" the paramedic

driving shouted back. The other was monitoring her vitals, her blood pressure, shining a light in Laura's eyes.

"Radio ahead. Tell them to get an OR prepped for an emergency C-section. I want everything ready and standing by for when we pull in, and have them call the blood bank, too. I want her typed and cross-matched. Andy, what's Laura's blood type?"

"O negative. What's going on?" Andy was holding his daughter. She was so tiny he was afraid of hurting her. Watching Laura, he could feel her slipping away, and for the first time, fear of losing her, of his daughter losing her mother, had him feeling a sense of helplessness he'd never once in his life experienced before.

"Dammit, prolapsed cord. Get her legs up. Laura, this is going to hurt, but I have to keep the baby off the cord."

"Ohh!" she screamed and cried as the paramedic held her leg back and the doctor put her hand in. There was blood everywhere.

"Laura, it's okay. Hold my hand." Andy slipped his hand in hers. It was weak; she could barely hold him.

The sirens blared, and the ambulance braked and pulled into the hospital. The back door opened, and emergency room nurses and doctors, all gowned up, were there waiting. The doctor was shouting orders, her hand still inside Laura as the gurney was lowered down. Andy climbed out and followed, carrying his daughter wrapped in a towel. A nurse grabbed his arm and brought him into a room filled with equipment.

"Let's get a look at that baby," a nurse said, taking the baby from Andy and setting her on the small bed.

Andy looked around. "Where's my wife?" he shouted.

A slim, blond-haired doctor with pink scrubs and glasses said, "Your wife's on the way to the OR for an emergency C-Section."

"I need to be there. I promised her I wouldn't leave her." Andy was frantic. "I want to make sure no one comes near my daughter or tries to take her."

"Sir, everything is going to be fine. Your daughter's small. She's got great breath sounds for a preemie, four pounds and six ounces. Let's get her in a warming bed and up to the neonatal unit and monitor her. You can follow your daughter up there."

Andy couldn't leave his daughter. He watched as they fastened an ID bracelet on her ankle and then followed the nurse and doctor to the elevator. He froze when he glimpsed Dr. Richardson heading straight for him with an expression of concern on her face. His only thought was that if that woman took one more step toward his baby or him, he'd put his hands on her.

"Stop right there. Do not come near my baby or Laura. Why are you here?" Andy growled, and the doctor appeared to stumble just as the elevator dinged.

"Mister Friessen, we need to take your daughter up." The young doctor beside his baby pushed the small bed his daughter was in onto the elevator with the nurse. Andy stepped in, and Dr. Richardson put her hand on the door.

"I need to talk to you, Andy. I don't know what's going on, but I think there may be a misunderstanding some-where. My God, I am a doctor, and my patient and her babies are my primary concern."

"You mean doing a C-section that you planned with my mother, taking our babies and not letting Laura see them? I mean to have your medical license revoked and you sent to jail," Andy barked.

"Doctor Richardson, I'm not sure what's going on here, but we need to go." The young doctor had a look on her face that was scared and alarmed. Andy could only presume she was terrified of him and maybe wondering what kind of paranoid nutcase he was, but then, they didn't know the whole story.

"I would never do anything like that. I have no idea who told you something that sick...."

"My wife heard you with my mother. She was so upset that she snuck out, thinking and believing that I had some part in it. But what convinced me was the nursery."

Dr. Richardson's face paled, and she stepped back as the elevator door slid closed. Andy wanted to pound the elevator door and yell and scream, but he didn't, as a few seconds later, the elevator door opened and he followed his daughter into the neonatal unit, where they put her on a warming bed and cleaned her up.

Andy was waiting for Laura in the private room they'd just moved her to. The babies were in the nursery, a son and a daughter. He still couldn't believe it. Laura had lost a fair amount of blood but hadn't needed a transfusion, as they quickly got the bleeding under control after the emergency C-section, where they delivered his son.

His baby boy was smaller, at four pounds three ounces, but he was doing well with his sister, both breathing on their own. When Dr. Richardson had shown up, he felt the icy chill and worry that Laura had screamed and cried and worried over, so he'd called Brian, his private detective, and ordered him down there. Brian was now standing outside the nursery, making sure no one went anywhere without his permission. Maybe he was being paranoid, but after what happened last night, with Laura sneaking out, finding the nursery, hearing her unbelievable story, he wasn't about to take any chances. Right now, he still needed to speak with Dr. Richardson, find out what kind of sneaky shit that woman was involved in.

Dr. Caldwell softly tapped on the door and stepped into the room. She was wearing blue scrubs, and her hair was sticking out here and there from the ponytail she had shoved it in. "How's she doing?" She grabbed the chart at the foot of the bed and perused the notes the nurses had scribbled.

"She hasn't woken up. Should I be worried?" Andy asked, and he was sure he was doing a damn poor job of hiding his feelings.

"No, everything looks good." She stepped around the side of the bed and pulled a penlight from the pocket above her breast. She opened Laura's eyelid and shone the light, and Laura flinched. Then she moved her hand and groaned.

Andy was on his feet right beside her, touching her face, her arm, her hand. "Hey, come on. Wake up, sleepy-head. Laura, it's a boy. We have a son and a daughter. They're both doing well."

She blinked and slowly opened her eyes to Andy's voice, smiling at him groggily. Then her eyes widened, and her expression changed to something he thought was terror as she reached for him and tried to move. "Andy, where are our babies?" she cried out.

"Shh, it's okay. They're fine. They're in the nursery just down the hall. I have someone watching them. He's not letting anyone near them." Andy smoothed her hair back, and she watched him and then let out a breath, something that sounded like relief. Even the shadow of fear that had flickered around her eyes relaxed. She nodded.

Dr. Caldwell was watching Andy with a look that seemed puzzled when he glanced up. "Andy, can I have a word with you?" She gestured toward the door. Obviously, being as sharp as he was, even when he was so damn tired, he realized that whatever it was, she didn't want it being said in front of Laura.

"Yeah," he said, but Laura seemed unwilling to let go of his hand. "Hey, I'll be right back. Everything's fine."

Laura was still so pale, and she tried to move onto her side. The IV tubing stuck out of her hand, and she winced.

"Laura, I'm going to have the nurse come in and give you something for the pain," Dr. Caldwell said.

"I don't want to go to sleep again. Nothing strong, please. Andy, don't let them put me out," Laura muttered. She really was depending on him.

"Laura, you're getting something to stop the hurting, okay? You just had major surgery. I'll make sure they don't knock you out." He pulled away and then leaned down and kissed her. "I'll be right back."

He strode to the door and stepped out in the hall to where Dr. Richardson was standing with a tall, dark-haired man wearing glasses and a suit. "What the hell is this?" He shot an accusing glance at Dr. Caldwell, a look that usually had people cowering in front of him. But not her, she merely crossed her arms as if intimidation by strong alpha-male types was something so old and done that she gave it no attention at all anymore.

"There is something you need to hear." Dr. Caldwell gestured toward Dr. Richardson.

"Andy, this is Michael Tanner. He is the chief counsel for the hospital," Dr. Richardson said. "After your accusation at the elevator that I would behave unethically, I thought it would be wise to bring Michael in."

"Well, you are right about one thing. You need a hell of a good lawyer with what you were plotting with my mother," Andy snapped, and a few passing nurses turned and watched. Andy knew they were probably trying to hear what was going on, but then, everyone on the floor knew something was up, especially when his hired man showed up outside the neonatal unit where his babies were and told the head nurse that if she had a problem with it, she could call security. She did, but security was more than willing, after hearing Andy Friessen's name, to allow the man to stay.

"Mister Friessen, I think there may be a misunderstanding here. Doctor Richardson showed me that your wife signed over all rights to the baby, in effect terminating her parental rights and saying she wished to not see the babies after they were born." The lawyer handed over a notarized document to Andy. When he stared down at Laura's neat, legible signature, he couldn't get one intelligent word to form in his brain.

"I was served this by your family lawyer," Dr. Richardson said. "When I called, he advised me that Laura chose money, a rather large amount, in exchange for walking away. She didn't want to discuss it. I never asked Laura. Frankly, I was disappointed that she found it so easy to just walk away." Dr. Richardson didn't move, and she spoke with such conviction that Andy could only wipe his open mouth roughly with his hand and then pump his hand into a fist once, twice, stifling the urge to drive his fist through the wall behind him.

"My wife did not sign this. She wouldn't have signed something like this," Andy said as he waved the papers in the air.

"Is that not her signature?" the lawyer asked.

Andy folded the legal document and stuffed it in his back pocket. "Excuse me. I think maybe it's time I call my lawyer." He hurried to the nurse's station. "I need to use your phone."

The older, dark-haired nurse behind the counter shook

her head. "Sir, I'm sorry. You'll have to use the payphone at the end of the hall."

"Let him use the phone, Donna." It was Dr. Richardson who spoke up, and then she said to Andy, "I think there is more going on here than both of us realize. I hope you find out the truth, Andy. The fact is that I like Laura, and I like you." Then she walked away.

The phone was set on the counter for Andy. He dialed, and the number was answered on the first ring, as if they were sitting and waiting by the phone.

"Jed, it's Andy. Diana awake?"

"She's still asleep. The first thing she's going to ask when she wakes up is about the babies." Andy could hear Gabriel and Danny in the background, and then Jed saying something to them. "The kids are awake, and Gabriel is a little worried, keeps asking for you and saying something about a wicked witch?"

"I'll talk to Gabriel later, but first, we have a boy and a girl. They're small but both doing good. But we have problem I need Diana for. There is a lawyer that showed up with Doctor Richardson, the hospital lawyer. They have a termination of parental rights apparently signed by Laura, and it's her signature on it."

Andy could hear only the clatter of dishes in the background and then Jed's heavy sigh.

"I'll wake Diana. We'll be right down."

Andy handed the phone back to the nurse and headed back to Laura's room. When he stepped inside, the bed was empty, and he was about to yell and demand someone tell him where she was when he heard a toilet flush and the bathroom door open. Laura stepped out with a nurse at her side, wheeling the IV rail, with Laura holding her abdomen as she shuffled her feet as if she were ninety years old.

"Hey, how're you doing?" Andy slid his arm around her and helped her back to bed.

"Just gave your wife a couple of Tylenol 3s. They're strong, but it'll only dull the pain. She won't take anything stronger."

Laura looked to Andy for help. She had dark circles under her eyes, and she took his hand, looking like she was about to fall over. "I want to see my babies."

"You bet." He glanced at the nurse, who nodded her head.

"I'll get a wheelchair, and you can take her down."

The nurse was out the door, and Andy sat on the bed beside her.

"Laura, I need to ask you something. Did you ever sign something for my mother? Anything recently?"

She frowned. "Andy, I haven't spoken with your mother. Why would I sign anything?"

"Well, I was just handed this." He pulled it from his back pocket and unfolded the paper, showing her the signature.

She reached a shaky hand for the legal document. "What the hell is this, Andy? Termination of rights, I...I don't understand?" She had a wild-eyed look, and even his touch didn't calm her. She looked about ready to claw out someone's eyes.

"Is that your signature, Laura?" Andy asked, pointing to the neat script that hadn't been copied but done in fresh blue ink.

"It looks like it, but I never signed anything like this." She jammed her fingers in her hair and tried to scoot off the bed.

"I've already called Jed. He's waking Diana. They're on their way down. How did your signature get on this?

Did anyone have you sign anything recently? Think, Laura. I know you're tired."

Laura shut her eyes, and tears popped out and slid down her cheek. "Just some healthcare forms Jules said you..." She weaved on the bed, and Andy slid his arm around her and laid her back in bed. He pushed the button to raise the head.

"What healthcare forms, and when was this?"

"I don't know. It was a while ago. It was a few days after I was back at the mansion. Jules brought me lunch, and I'd just woken up; she had an envelope and pulled some papers out and said that they were for healthcare, to make sure I was covered under you, to cover the doctor. I just signed, Andy. Jules held the paper and turned the pages, and I signed where she said. I didn't read anything. I thought you sent her up?"

"I would never send anyone up, especially a servant, to have you sign anything. And healthcare, I take care of all that for you." Andy was irritated and stung by betrayal. He couldn't believe Jules would do something this despicable to his wife. Hell, she'd all but raised him. She was like family. Why would she do this to him? To Laura?

There was a tap on the door, and the nurse pushed a wheelchair inside. "Okay, Mister Friessen, do you want to help your wife and take her down to see your babies?"

"I do. Ready?" he asked her, then helped her up and lifted her into the chair. The nurse put a cotton blanket over Laura's legs, and Andy pushed her out of the room and to the nursery, to the two tiny infants side by side with the nametags taped to the clear plastic, baby boy and baby girl Friessen. A nurse lifted a baby each to both Andy and Laura.

"Oh my God, Laura," Andy said. "They're absolutely beautiful."

Twenty~Five

Laura was doing her best to nurse the babies, with a pillow across her lap and the lactation consultant still in the room. She finally had both babies latched on a breast at the same time. It had been three days since Jeremy and Chelsea were born, three days since all hell had broken loose at the Friessen mansion, at the hospital, and three days since Andy walked away from the family he'd been born into, stood side by side with, honored, and blindly belonged to. The Friessens were about family, blood lines, looking after your own, and belonging. It was just that his family, namely Todd, and Caroline, who his father had married, had brought in greed and power, aligning their families through marriage.

Laura had woken to Diana, her lawyer and now Andy's lawyer, telling her not to worry, she'd look after everything, and Jed hovering like the overprotective husband he was.

Andy hadn't shared too much the last few days, just that he'd handled everything, and he repeatedly told her not to worry, which was comforting, considering the only thing she wanted to do each time she woke up was hold her babies and see Gabriel. She didn't have the energy to face what she realized was a hornets' nest. Today, Dr. Caldwell had said she could go home, but she had to have help.

Andy said nothing. He took the information of what they needed for the babies and said he'd handle that, too, so when Jeremy fell asleep at her breast first, then Chelsea, Laura was at a loss of what to do. Andy had helped up until now, taking one of the babies and burping them. She worried for a second about how she was going to do this, how she'd manage at all without him right now.

"One at a time. Burp one, then the other." The nice lady stepped closer and lifted one of the babies from Laura.

The hospital room door opened, and Andy stepped inside. "So I guess the day is here. Are you sure you're up to leaving, Laura?" He approached the older lady who held his son and scooped him into his arms. "Look at you. I think he has your nose, Laura. Just wait until I get you your first pony."

"Andy, he needs to walk first, and don't forget your daughter. Maybe she'd like a pony, too," Laura said as she held Chelsea, watching the joy on her husband's face.

Another nurse stepped into the room with a clipboard. "Mister Friessen, would you like to sign for your wife's release. Then, if you can bring up the car seats, we'll help you get the babies settled and ready to leave."

Andy took the clipboard one handed and read through the paperwork. With the nurse holding the clipboard again, he scribbled his name.

Laura didn't have a chance to think or worry or wonder about anything as she dressed in the comfortable sweatpants, t-shirt, and jacket Andy had brought. By the time she was ready, he had both babies buckled into their car seats, and he carried both car seats out of the hospital and secured them into the backseat of the truck, then helped Laura in.

She never asked where they were going, because she just assumed they were going back to Jed and Diana's, but when her brain finally clicked and registered they were going the wrong way, she glanced over at her husband and asked, "Andy, where are we going?"

He didn't look at her as he drove down the highway headed toward the Friessen mansion. "We're going home, Laura."

She started sputtering and couldn't seem to form one reasonable word. She wanted to demand that he stop and turn around, and she was about to yell when he signaled at a dirt driveway right before a crop of oak trees and turned down the tree-lined driveway, pulling up to a lovely two-story house painted gray with white trim. Jed's truck just happened to be parked in front.

Diana waved from the lovely covered porch that appeared to wrap around the front of the house. Laura didn't realize that Andy had stopped and shut off the engine until he opened her door.

"Andy, whose house is this?"

Andy unbuckled her seat belt and reached around her waist, lifting her out and setting her down. "It's ours."

Gabriel raced from around the side of the house, Danny running after him, his tiny little legs pumping, and Jed followed. Andy lifted Gabriel in his arms, and when he reached for Laura, grinning ear to ear, she held out her arms to take him.

"No way, bud. Your mom is doing no lifting for a while yet, so you're going to have to make do with me."

"Andy, I don't know what to say. How did you...?" She put her hands on her head and just stared at the beautiful square home with a peaked roof and windows everywhere. It was a home from her dreams, but she couldn't figure out what he meant by it being theirs.

Andy slid his arm around her shoulder. "Go in and take a look. I bought it for us. Had to move mountains to make it happen so quickly, but it was already empty. The owners left it furnished. They were planning on selling off the furnishings anyways, as they've retired and have a place in Arizona. The title still has to clear, but it's just ours, no servants, no mansion, just a small house."

Laura threw her arms around him and was rocked by the wave of emotions, joy, happiness, everything, and she couldn't stop the tears as she pressed her face into Andy's chest.

"I thought you'd be happy?" Andy said as he held her with his one arm, the other holding Gabriel.

"I am so happy. I can't believe you did this. I just wanted a house for us, our own place, and you did this...." Laura gazed up at Andy as Gabriel patted her cheek. "I love you," she said.

Andy leaned down and kissed her. "Why don't you go on in the house? Diana's inside. I'll bring the babies in."

"Hey, you, why don't you come with me?" Jed reached for Gabriel. "Come on, Laura. I'll walk you in. I hope you don't mind, but Diana took charge of getting some things ready for you."

"Why would I mind? I can't believe this, Jed. This is a dream. It's all I wanted, just something for us."

Andy paused outside the door and watched Jed, who herded both kids inside and held the screen door open for Laura. And he smiled.

Twenty-Six

The babies were upstairs in the nursery, sleeping after Laura had nursed them. Jed had hired a local woman and her husband to set up the cribs and organize the nursery for them. He'd also hired the woman's daughter to stay and help Laura for the next few weeks with the babies, with Gabriel, and with the house. She'd been greeted by the young lady, who was closer to Laura's age and who'd helped get the babies settled while Diana showed Laura her new house. It had five bedrooms, two full bathrooms, a living room, and an open kitchen.

It was a comfortable home, and Laura felt herself sighing in relief when she didn't see one useless trinket anywhere. She yawned, holding the mug of green tea that Diana had just poured for her.

"You should really go lie down, Laura, get some sleep." Diana sat across from her and leaned back in the armchair at the kitchen table, running her hand over her large, swollen belly.

"I will soon. I wanted to talk to you. This is all so surreal. I still can't believe Andy did this. I don't know if he has any idea what it means to me to have my own home, our home. Just us and our kids. I never expected this." Laura sipped on her tea and studied Diana, who had dark smudges under her eyes. She looked so tired. "You feeling okay, Diana? You look really worn out."

"Oh, you know how it is at the end—the last few weeks. I just haven't been sleeping well. I'm ready to have this baby, though."

"I know you've done a lot to help us, and I hope it didn't put too much of a burden on you, especially now, and you and Jed looking after Gabriel, and what you did here. Diana, I owe you so much."

"You owe me nothing, honey. We're family, in an odd sort of way, and your turn will come. Besides, I'm real happy to see you and Andy together and having worked things out. He loves you, and I don't think I've ever seen him so unburdened, so happy." Diana watched Jed and Andy out in the yard with Gabriel and Danny. The two men were talking and laughing.

"Diana, what happened?"

Diana jerked her gaze back to Laura and frowned. "What are you talking about?"

"Andy wouldn't tell me anything. I think he was trying to protect me. But there was that legal document where I supposedly signed away my rights. I told Andy that the only thing I remembered signing were those forms from Jules. Now we're here. What about Doctor Richardson and Caroline?" She gestured with her hand and moved uncomfortably in her seat.

"Oh, I see. Well, for one, Andy is a Friessen man, and they like to hide things from us. I know they honestly believe they are protecting us by keeping us in the dark. You know this, and you've really got a better chance of taming a black bear than you do of getting our men to change, so you're going to have to get smart and accept some things. When you can't, figure a way to come at it in a different direction."

She laughed softly, and then a shadow of worry filled her expression. "Jules swore she didn't know what you were signing. She said Caroline gave her the papers, said they were some medical documents that Andy forgot to get you to sign, and every page had already been marked for where you were to sign. But we don't know for sure. In all fairness, I don't think she realized the lengths that Caroline would go to. Caroline's lawyer who prepared the documents can't and won't speak to us, and he did nothing wrong, as he didn't have you sign or participate in any way that makes him accountable. Caroline says that she gave the documents to Jules, and Jules had you sign them knowing full well they were to terminate your rights. It came down to Jules' word against Caroline's.

"Jules quit, by the way. She was devastated, and Andy refused to pursue it with her. He dropped the matter on my recommendation. Apparently, a few of the staff did quit once they heard of this, but you can't get Caroline for anything on this; she's too slick. Besides, the documents have been voided, shredded, and were never filed with the court." Diana gazed out the window again. A darkness appeared in her expression that Laura could only put to some skeletons or something hurtful Diana was holding on to.

"Diana, you've never told me about your past with Andy," Laura said. She watched Diana's face pale as she firmed her lips.

"Sometimes what's in your past is so painful and filled with hurt that it's best left there. My past with Andy is buried and done, and that's where it needs to stay. Besides, just watching Andy here, and when he told Jed what he was doing, buying this place, we couldn't believe he was walking away from everything he's ever known. We're proud of him, and so should you be. Put everything behind you. You should know Doctor Richardson was absolved of any wrongdoing. She did follow the letter of the law with the termination of parental rights. She won't speak with me, but my doctor said she's ethical. She's known her for years, so I believe she didn't know the truth. She should have asked you, in all fairness, but I also believe what she said to Andy, that she was disappointed in you; that you'd be willing to walk away so easily for money." Diana gestured her uncertainty with her hands. "Oh, it looks like we're about to be invaded."

The kids, Jed, and Andy clomped in the front door, everyone making a beeline for the kitchen.

"Kids are hungry," Jed said.

Diana and Laura exchanged a look and then burst out laughing.

"Andy, what about Aida?" Laura slid the green and white duvet back from the queen-size bed in their comfortable bedroom, with an oak dresser and mirror, a chest of drawers, and a closet. It was just a bedroom, no walk-in closet, no fireplace, no extravagance, and she'd wondered for a moment if Andy would miss all that.

"Come on, get in bed. You're about to fall over." Andy was standing right in front of her in jeans and a plaid shirt. His jaw was scruffy, as he hadn't shaved for a few days. Did the man have any idea how much she loved that look?

Laura was still in the sweatpants and t-shirt she'd worn home from the hospital, and she eased onto the bed and scooted down as Andy covered her. It was late afternoon, and Diana and Jed had just left with Danny. Andy had noticed Laura's head weaving a bit while she sat at the kitchen table with her eyes shut, and he had lifted her in his arms and carried her upstairs to bed.

"Andy, I'm worried about Aida. You didn't tell me about Jules and some of the other staff quitting."

He was leaning over, his arms braced on either side of her, and his scent was so him that she just wanted to pull him beside her and curl up into him. She touched his face, and Andy pressed a kiss into her palm.

"I'll go see Aida. I'll make sure she's okay, but I want you to get some sleep. You're just out of the hospital."

"Andy, I can't hear the babies. Can you get a baby monitor?" she asked in a panic. Even though there was someone here to help watch over her babies, she needed to be able to hear them before she could rest.

"I've got a monitor, but let Jenny get the babies. I'll take Gabriel with me to see Aida. Jenny is only here during the day. She's got it now, and we'll have it tonight. Sleep now while you can." Andy kissed Laura again.

"Andy?"

He stopped and gave her one of those exasperated looks as he tapped his hand on the doorframe.

"You don't have to protect me so much. Are you ever going to tell me what happened with Caroline?"

"Well, that's where you're wrong, Laura. I do need to protect you, and the only thing you need to know is that it's over with what my mother did and with everyone involved. I've handled it. I'm your husband, and if anyone tries to pull any underhanded shit against you, to hurt you, I will deal with it. That is my right, and I will always take care of my family."

Wow. Talk about saying all the right things. Did he have any idea how important it was to her to hear that? Slaying her dragons, fighting her fights, taking care of his family, her. *My God* was all she could think as she said, "Okay."

The passion that oozed from him, the way he tightened up as if ready to stand guard and fight Caroline, the doctor, the lawyers for her was him showing her she wasn't a nuisance, an irritation. She was important to him. Without a doubt, she knew, that in his way, he loved her, he loved Gabriel, and he loved his babies. Her husband, Andy Friessen, was a difficult man, a hard man, a strong man whom she'd never ever be able to bend to her will, but he was a man who'd always keep her on her toes, a man she loved more than her next breath.

"Go to sleep," he said as he pulled the door closed, and she listened to his footsteps, Gabriel's excitement, and the young girl who was watching her babies. For the first time, she felt peace.

Twenty~Eight

ndy glanced in the rear-view mirror. Gabriel was grinning ear to ear in the backseat of his pickup; his bangs were drooping in his eyes. Maybe tomorrow Andy would take him and the two of them could get a haircut. Andy braked at the end of his driveway and glanced back at his home. Forty acres, with a small, two-stall barn in back, a corral, some pasture—a basic, modest home he'd never once pictured himself living in. He couldn't quite shake this sense of it being "his" and "their" home. No one was going to show up here and turn their life upside down, because for the first time in his life, he'd walked away from his family, who they were, what they were, and all that power. He hadn't even considered calling Todd, whom he hadn't heard from since marrying Laura. No, that was a closed chapter. Everything he did from this day forward would be his: the money he made, his property, his house. It was a way of life, and whatever he did, he would no longer be running or cleaning up anything for Todd or on behalf of the Friessens. His family came first, and everything he did would be for his family, Laura, Gabriel, Chelsea, and Jeremy. Maybe, for the first time, he understood Jed a little better.

Andy signaled and turned onto the highway, driving into town and parking in front of Aida's modest bungalow. Gabriel waited for Andy to lift him out and then held his hand while he led him up the steps.

Andy noticed everything was dark and wondered if she was home. He tapped on the door. There was nothing, no footsteps, so he knocked harder, rattling the screen door.

"Where's Aida?" Gabriel asked.

"I don't know, bud. Let's go around back and see if her car's here."

Gabriel hopped down the front steps and ran around the side of the house to the white picket fence in back. Andy opened the gate and went to the single car garage behind the house. He looked in the window and spotted her car inside. Gabriel was hopping up and down, trying to see through the window where Andy was looking.

"Just stay down, bud." Andy tried to turn the knob and open the garage door, but it was locked. "Aida, where are you? Maybe she's sleeping."

Andy yanked his cell phone from his pocket and dialed Aida's number. He could hear the phone ringing from where he stood in the backyard. He listened to the ring echo through the house, but there was no other sound, no footsteps, no rustling, nothing.

"Come on, Aida, where are you? Maybe she went out for a walk," Andy said to Gabriel, who was watching him and waiting.

Andy hated to leave. He needed to see Aida, make sure she was okay, not just for Laura but because Andy admired her so much. She really was one of the few who'd always been in Laura's corner and didn't give a rat's ass what other people thought, especially him. After all hell had broken loose two days ago, when he appeared with the sheriff and Diana and Jed, who'd questioned Jules as she cried and shrieked over what she'd done, Aida had pulled him aside and questioned him on Caroline.

The woman had been furious, but she hadn't said one word. She'd tossed her hairnet and apron on the counter, patted Andy on the arm, and said, "You look after that girl and Gabriel. Don't bring them back here. It's time you struck out on your own. Make your own way. Laura and Gabriel and those babies are your family, your only responsibility now. Keep them out of this life and far away from your family." Then she'd grabbed her purse and left. He knew she had quit, and he'd taken what she said to heart, calling a local realtor who'd found their house, a little acreage, and set in motion what he'd already decided to do. But the fact was that Aida had a way of putting him on a path and in a direction driven entirely by his conscience.

Andy stepped onto the small back deck and started looking through the windows. The curtains were old lace and somewhat transparent. He wasn't sure, but he thought he saw someone sitting in a rocker. Andy put his face to the pane glass, his hand shading his eyes to cut through the reflection.

Andy opened the screen door and pounded again, yelling, "Aida!" Then he went back to the window and peeked in. There was no movement, and something unsettling squeezed inside of him. "Gabriel, go down the stairs on the grass for just a second."

Gabriel grabbed his leg and held on. "No, Andy, don't leave me."

Andy bent down and held Gabriel's shoulders, "Hey, listen to me. I am not leaving you. I just need you to stay back. You know I'll always look after you. I won't let anything happen to you."

But Gabriel wouldn't let go of his leg. There was no way Gabriel was taking one step down without Andy.

"Okay, just stand here." He put Gabriel beside him on the other side of the door, and the boy seemed okay with that.

Andy put his shoulder to the door. With a tight grip on the handle, he rammed his shoulder, pounding it against the door. Again he slammed it hard until it gave, the wood splintering around the bolt as he stumbled in.

He held his hand out to Gabriel. "Just stay here for a minute until I call you."

Gabriel was standing in the doorway, wide-eyed.

Andy pointed a finger sharply at Gabriel and gave him a stern look, and he stayed right where he was, looking up at Andy with a look that told Andy how much he depended on him for everything.

Andy stepped cautiously through the kitchen, sniffing the air and something foul. He spotted a piece of meat on the counter with flies swarming. Then he stepped into a small dining area with a small, round table and four chairs. "Aida?" he called out again as he looked into the living room and to a rocker where Aida was sitting. Her wrinkled hands rested on the arms of the chair, and her head was slouched to the side, her mouth open.

Andy shut his eyes and tried to tell his heart it would be okay, but that didn't stop the wave of emotions that was pounding at him. He pressed his hand to her neck, but there was nothing, no pulse, and even touching the wrinkled skin had his senses screaming that it wasn't quite right. There was no life, but he already knew she was dead by her eyes. Everything that had stoked that woman was gone. The whites were gray, and the life that had once shot fire at him with one glance was cloudy and distant. Not an ounce of anything was left there. Andy squatted down in front of the old woman and pressed the back of his wrist to his mouth as he blinked back tears. How in the hell was he going to tell Laura? She'd be devastated.

"Andy," Gabriel called to him from the back door, and he heard the floor squeak. He didn't miss the fear in Gabriel's voice.

"Stay there, Gabriel." Andy couldn't do anything for Aida, and he couldn't let Gabriel see her, not like this. He yanked his cell phone out as he strode with a heavy heart to the back door, where Gabriel was trying to peek around the corner. He placed his hand on Gabriel's shoulder. "Outside, Gabriel. Come with me."

He stood outside with Gabriel on the grass, and the little boy wouldn't leave his side as he dialed emergency, giving Aida's address. He was careful to keep his back to Gabriel, to not look at him. When he hung up, he pressed the phone to his forehead, and the boy he thought of as his son was so quiet. Of course, he knew something was wrong, and when he glanced down, there were tears in his innocent blue eyes. All Andy did was lean down and take him in his arms, saying, "I'm so sorry." And he let him cry.

He didn't know how long they'd been there, but he figured it was about an hour as they stood outside. He spoke with a new deputy, a stocky blond guy. The coroner was just wrapping up, and they'd taken Aida out the front door. Apparently, Aida had been dead for two days. Heart attack was what the coroner said she suspected. Andy had wanted to call Jed, but he stopped before he finished dialing. He couldn't do that to Jed. He had Diana to look after, and she was due any day. He'd seen how tired she was. The two of them had been there for Andy and Laura for days, helping to clean up and make sense of the mess his mother had created.

"Andy Friessen?" the deputy called to him from the back door. Andy knew Gabriel was terrified, and he needed to get home, to get him away from this horrid scene that was difficult for most adults to process.

"Yes, what is it?"

"Found something with your name on it." The deputy gestured for him to come in.

One look at Gabriel's lost expression had Andy lifting him in his arms. "We're going home after this, okay? Everything's fine."

Gabriel said nothing but rested his head on Andy's shoulder as he walked into the house behind the deputy. He noticed the rotted piece of meat was now gone.

"We found this on table with your name on it." The deputy held out a brown envelope, the kind that had bubble wrap inside.

Andy hesitated a second before taking the envelope. For the life of him, he couldn't figure out what Aida would have left for him. "I'm taking my kid home now. I gave you my number, so if you need anything, you can call me."

The deputy flushed with an expression that appeared so much like sympathy as he gazed at Gabriel. "We're just about done here. I'll call you after I hear from the coroner, but it looks like she went peacefully."

Andy could only nod as his throat thickened with emotion. He left, carrying Gabriel out the back door, the envelope in his hand.

Laura had been awake when he got home. She was in their cozy living room, nursing the babies. Dinner was ready, but he'd long since lost his appetite.

Jenny was in the kitchen, lifting a steaming casserole out of the oven. "My mom sent this over," she said.

"Thanks, Jenny. That'll be all for tonight. Why don't you head on home before it gets dark?"

Gabriel was still in his arms as he held the door open for the young lady as she pulled her coat on.

"What time would you like me to come in the morning?"

"How about ten?"

She nodded and hopped down the steps and toward the path that led to her parents' neighboring property.

Gabriel's head was still pressed against Andy's shoulder and into his neck, and Laura was frowning from where she rocked one of the babies. The other was now nestled in a bassinet beside the rocker.

"What's going on, Andy? Is something wrong?"

She was so perceptive, and his jaw was clamped together so hard it had begun to ache. He rubbed Gabriel's back and then put him down.

"Hey, listen, I want to talk to your mom a minute. Can you run upstairs to the bathroom and wash your hands for dinner?" Andy went down on one knee in front of him. Gabriel said nothing, but the sadness in his eyes tore at Andy's heart. He wanted to make it better, to take away that hurt and put back the joy that had flickered from his eyes and just this morning had lit up his entire face. But he couldn't. "You're my big boy. Come on, get going."

And Gabriel did. He climbed up the stairs, and Andy waited until he was in the bathroom before sitting on the stool in front of Laura. He peeked at his son, who was in her arms and now sound asleep. When he looked up at her, she was watching him with fear and uncertainty.

"Something happened when I went to Aida's." He cleared his throat and glanced away to pull himself together.

"Andy, you're scaring me." Her voice trembled.

Andy reached over and scooped the baby from her arms, putting him in the bassinet beside his sister. Then he took both of Laura's hands in his. "Laura, Aida had a heart attack and died. I found her in her rocker."

Laura was crying, and Andy pulled her onto his lap. She must have known she was scaring Gabriel, as she tucked her face into his chest to muffle her sobs. Andy spotted Gabriel hovering on the steps. "Come on down, bud. Your mom's a little sad. I had to tell her about Aida." Andy reached his hand out to Gabriel, and the little boy hurried down the stairs and into Andy's other arm. Laura reached out and touched her little boy's shoulder, then looked up at Andy with red, swollen eyes.

"Andy, she was all I had for family. She was like a mother to me."

"I know. But you're wrong. I'm your family. We're a family, you and me, Gabriel and Chelsea and Jeremy. All of us, Laura. Aida—I'm so sorry, honey."

"What's going to happen to her? Where is she?"

"She's at the morgue, and I never asked her if she had family." Andy held Laura and Gabriel and could have kicked himself as he realized he never wanted to get too personal with the staff.

"I don't know what happened to them, Andy, but I know she told me that she'd lost her family years ago. She wouldn't talk about it, just said it is what it is. You know Aida; if she didn't want to talk, she didn't."

Andy laughed softly under his breath, but it was far from joyful. There was something about Aida where she could have made him do anything and feel guilty for all of his shortcomings at the same time. She had been the only person he needed to respect him. For the life of him, he didn't know why it had mattered so much.

"Andy, we can't leave her there if she has no family who is going to look after a funeral, getting her clothes, burying her, saying goodbye."

"I'll handle it. I'll take care of all the arrangements. I don't want you to worry about it." Andy kissed Laura on the top of her head. "Come on, let's go have dinner."

Laura slid off his knee, and Andy supported her arm while she stood up. "I'm not hungry, Andy. I don't think I can eat."

Andy lifted Gabriel in his arms and stood up. "You have to, Laura; you're nursing. Come on. I bet you're hungry, too, Gabriel?"

But he just shook his head. Andy ushered Laura into the kitchen and sat Gabriel in one of the chairs. "Come on, let's see what's for dinner. I'm sure once we taste it, we'll all realize how hungry we are." Andy lifted the tin foil from the casserole dish that was sitting on a hot mitt beside the stove. "Mmm, shepherd's pie smells good."

Laura was looking lost, and her eyes were red rimmed as she stared at Andy.

"Laura, get some plates." He gestured with his head to Gabriel. It took Laura a second, but then she understood what he was saying, and she nodded and forced a pathetic smile to her lips, grabbing three plates from the cupboard. The three of them picked at their first dinner, which should have been filled with joy, celebration, and excitement, but instead was shadowed and filled with the emptiness of the passing of someone they'd all loved and who had been so much a part of Andy and Laura.

LAURA FELT an unbearable sense of loss. All the excitement and love she felt for Andy, for their new life, and today— well, her heart felt as if it had been shattered.

She'd bathed the babies side by side with Andy, and she'd nursed them again, and now they were asleep in the bedroom beside theirs. The monitor was hooked up and sat in its holder beside the bed. She was nestled on her side, her hand resting under the pillow, and she listened to the background noises as Andy settled Gabriel and got him ready for bed.

She still couldn't believe what Andy had done, separating them from his family, starting a new life with just them. It was a dream, but her dream had also included a spot for Aida. She'd assumed the old woman would always be a part of their life.

Laura swiped at the tear that slid down the side of her

nose. She felt such a closeness to Andy and was surprised at how he'd become her everything. He was the father Gabriel deserved to have.

"We have to be real quiet. See your brother and sister sleeping? Well, you're their big brother, and you get to help me look after them and your mom, too."

"Where's Aida?"

Laura watched the monitor and held her breath, waiting for Andy to respond. She'd been so wrapped up in her own grief, tired and still recovering from the babies and surgery, that she'd left all of this to Andy, but he was making it so easy for her, and she loved him for that, especially for his broad shoulders, which held her and her son up and sheltered them from everything bad.

"Aida is now with the angels. She finished what she had to do here. Do you know what happens when you get old and die?" Andy asked her son, and she found herself listening and believing that he knew everything and exactly where Aida was now.

"No."

Laura jammed her fist into her mouth. Of course her little boy didn't know what death was. Thank God he'd never experienced it before.

"Well, we all come here, and we all have a purpose, something we need to do. When we're done, that's when we leave and go home. It's a wonderful place, surrounded by angels. And that's where Aida is. I like to think that she's watching over us now, happy and smiling because she just wanted our family, you and me, your mom, Chelsea and Jeremy, together and happy. She's always going to be with you. You have to close your eyes and think of a fun time with her, and she'll be right there."

"Can she see us now? Can she come back and visit?"

"No, she can't come back, but you can see her anytime

you want just by closing your eyes and remembering her face, remembering a happy time and how much she loved you."

Andy must have left the babies' room, as she couldn't hear him anymore. She stared at the monitor, her heart full of what he'd said. Laura had never had much faith and had certainly never spoken with Gabriel about angels, except Andy had made her heart lighter by what he'd just said about Aida.

"Hey, what are you still doing awake?" Andy strode into their bedroom in his stocking feet, his blue jeans hugging his hips, his silver belt buckle featured an engraved eagle. He sat beside her on the bed and swept his fingers through her hair.

Laura reached up and linked her fingers with his. "I heard what you said to Gabriel. I would never have come up with that. Do you really believe Aida is watching over us?"

He glanced away and squinted as if trying to think of something to say. "I do, Laura. Aida was a tough old bird, and she put up with absolutely no crap of mine and called me out any chance she got." Andy pulled his hand away. "Just believe it, Laura. I believe that she's happy for us and where we are now."

Laura watched something in Andy she hadn't seen before. It was love for her, and she truly believed he spoke from the heart by what he said.

He bent down and kissed her. "Go to sleep."

"Are you coming to bed?" she asked, rising up on her elbows when he started out of the room.

"Not quite yet. I have a few things to take care of."

"Are you okay, Andy?" He was carrying everything on his shoulders, but there was a shadow in his expression of something heavy, and all she could think of was that it was because of Aida. "I mean, you're handling all of this, and I want to help, Andy. I'm not being fair to you, letting you handle all of this."

"You listen to me: I'm fine. Don't worry about me. I'm looking after you and Gabriel. You go to sleep, because we could be up a few times tonight, and I can only help with part of it." Andy watched her for a minute before pulling the door partially closed and striding away; she listened to the squeak of the stairs as he climbed down.

"Thank you, Andy," she whispered. "I love you so much." She shut her eyes, feeling the weight of what she'd carried before lift away.

CHAPTER
Thirty

Andy held the sealed brown envelope in his hand. There wasn't anything stronger in the house to drink than lemonade, and right now he'd have killed for a shot of whiskey. Maybe tomorrow he'd rectify that, but tonight, as he sat in the kitchen, he slit the envelope open and pulled out a small recorder wrapped with a single sheet of paper.

He unfolded the stiff white paper and recognized Caroline's logo on the bottom of the page. But it wasn't his mother's writing. The clean, neat script was all Aida.

My dear Andy,

If you're reading this, then something has happened to me. It's cowardly on my part, but I've not been well for a while, and my old body has broken down on me. I don't have the fight I once did. I lost that years ago. Please keep Laura and dear Gabriel safe, and those precious babies.

I'm depending on you. I know you can do this. I was hard on you, but I could see in you a love for your family that I don't think you realized was there. Just love them, protect them. That's all they want.

When Laura left you, she cried for you every night. She thought I didn't know, as she tried to muffle her cries in her pillow. But I knew. Only someone who's been there and seen that, who has been beaten down, having lost everything because life decided to kick her in the head, could know what she felt. She's a good girl, and she loves you. Don't screw it up!

Andy rubbed his chin and couldn't help the laugh that only Aida could bring out of him. Even from her grave, she had a way of kicking him in the ass that he appreciated.

You'll see that I stuck a little recorder in there. Well, what you do with it is your decision. Only you can decide what to do with this. I'm sorry to sound so cryptic, but no one can tell any of us how we hold someone accountable or whether to forgive and walk away.

There are times when right and wrong isn't so black and white. Going into war and taking a fight on may end up hurting the ones you love and may not be as simple as you think. Take that from an old woman who's made every mistake and learned and lived with all the regrets and consequences of her actions.

So when you listen to this tape, it'll be your choice what do with it.

Bless you, Andy Friessen, and remember, whatever you decide, I'll not judge you. All I ask is that you'll forgive me.

Aida

Andy held the small recorder and turned it over in his hand, wondering what the hell the woman had on here. But this was Aida; what he'd come to expect from her was nothing short of the unexpected.

He pressed the play button and adjusted the volume. He could hear kitchen clatter and voices he didn't recognize, then rustling.

"Aida, you've been with this household for how many years?"

Andy felt his heart squeeze at the cold voice of his mother.

"Fifteen years," Aida said.

"Well, I'm trying to find out how loyal you are, Aida."

"Loyal. I do my job, Missus Friessen. I cook, and I stay out of your business."

"Ah, yes, you do that, which I much appreciate. There is one thing. Not much goes on that I don't know of, and that includes the past and present of anyone who works for me. It's important for me, shall we say, to stay current. Aida, you were the whore of a rich man. You got pregnant, and when he found out, he promised he'd marry you, do right by you, the foolish boy, but his family found out and took your child. They told him what he was to do, and you were left with nothing. Oh, you tried to see her, were even arrested. The last time, you served, what...?"

There was a clatter and a moment of silence.

"Ten years of hell on some trumped-up charge."

"Arizona has quite a reputation, doesn't it, Aida? What was it like, being locked in a cage twenty-three hours a day?"

"You're a cruel woman, Missus Friessen. What do you want?"

Andy couldn't believe what he was listening to, and he felt anger and rage burning on Aida's behalf. What the hell was his mother doing, digging up dirt on Aida? He didn't know any of this and shut his eyes at the horrible secret she'd carried, at the hell she'd lived through. He felt, for a moment, as if he was eavesdropping, and then his rage burned at how this could have happened. What had she been doing in jail? It couldn't be that easy, but he also knew that when people had money and power, they could make anything happen, especially to someone who didn't matter. For some reason, Aida had left this for him, and she wanted him to hear it. It was her story, but it was also something that could have happened to his wife. He'd never let that happen.

"If you're telling me you've hired someone to dig out all the dirt and skeletons from my closet, and for what purpose but your own kicks, it's beyond me, Missus Friessen, but if this is your way of getting rid of me, well, I'll save you the joy of firing me and bid you goodbye, and I quit."

"Oh, not so fast, Aida. I don't think it's in your best interest, since you violated your parole by leaving the state, even though you left the state—how many years ago was it now, Aida? Do you know what they do to parole violators in Arizona, even after all these years? Since it was kidnapping and extortion, they tend to throw away the key."

"You can't kidnap your own child, and there was no extortion, just a fancy lawyer and a family who bought witnesses to create the illusion of what they wanted."

Caroline laughed again. Andy recognized her trademark laugh. He'd heard it many times when she was holding on to something that would get her everything she wanted.

"Missus Friessen, what do you want?" Aida asked with a sharpness in her voice that Andy had not heard before.

"I want Laura gone, and you're going to help me. Andy may not realize it yet, but his father and I have plans for him, and he needs the right wife to make that happen. Laura just won't do, and she embarrassed me. I can't ever allow anyone to do that."

"I don't believe you have a say. Laura and Andy love each other. She is going to have his babies."

"Ah, yes, his babies. Well, that part has been taken care of. His babies will be nursed and raised as the Friessens they are. They'll soon have a new mother, and Laura and her bastard son will soon be a memory for Andy. Remember, Aida, how easy was it for your John? He promised he'd love you forever, that he'd marry you, and then he turned his back on you and went along with everything his family said. He never defended you."

"You're quite mistaken and don't know your son very well if you think he'd allow any of this to happen. Andy Friessen has a conscience; he knows right and wrong, and he'd not walk away from Laura. No one can tell that man what to do, not even you, Missus Friessen."

"Oh, I know my son well. Andy may be strong willed and might need the right encouragement. You are wrong about one thing—Andy will hate her, and he'll never want to see her again after he learns what she's done."

"Laura has done nothing wrong. What are you accusing her of? What have you done?"

"Oh, Andy will see that she sold her babies and walked away from him, from them, without a second thought for the right price, because money was more important to her, and I'll show Andy everything after she's gone. He may not believe me at first, but when he can't find her..."

"You're a fool if you think Laura would take money for her babies. She'd go to the grave fighting for her children. She won't walk away."

Andy heard his mother laugh again, and he glanced up and out into the living room, turning the sound down so Laura wouldn't be able to hear from upstairs.

"It won't be as easy to make her go away and disappear as it was with me."

"Well, that's where you're wrong, because you're going to convince her, and you're going to help her see that she needs to go away. You'll do this so that she doesn't suffer your same fate. Prisons swallow young women up all the time. What should it be, drugs, murder? Hmm, let me think. Ah, yes, after you return to your cage in Arizona, Laura will follow, and authorities in Arizona tend to throw the book at traffickers depending on the drug they find stuffed in their suitcases. She could be looking at ten, twelve, twenty years. And you know what happens in prisons to young, pretty things like Laura."

"Leave her alone. That girl is good and honest, and her little boy did nothing to deserve your spite. They have a good life, and Andy loves them." Aida's voice sounded old and weary, as if her energy had been stripped out of her.

"No, I don't think I will. Make your choice, Aida. You have twenty-four hours, and then I want your answer."

There was a rustle, and then the tape clicked off. There was static and then another click as he listened to someone's breathing and a scrape of a chair before Aida's voice came back on.

"Andy, we all have our skeletons. Please don't judge me. Your mother, well, I knew she was up to something, and I never wanted Laura to endure what I did. I survived. But my life is over. Her, you, Gabriel, and those babies, well, you're just at the beginning of your life together. I cannot go back to prison. I'd die there in that cell. The only crime I committed was loving the wrong man."

There was a heavy sigh, and Andy stared at the tape as he leaned on his elbows and jammed his fingers through his hair. He couldn't believe what he was listening to, what he heard from his mother. He felt his blood race through his veins as if he had been shocked by an electric current.

"I will not do what your mother asked. You already know, Andy, about the termination of rights. I spoke with you today when you showed up with that young sheriff. It scared the hell out of me, having him there. I thought right then that your mother would sell me out, as I'd not lived up to my end of the bargain. For a minute, I thought he'd be taking me away. In the end, I just couldn't do it and be able to look myself in the mirror.

"I never slept that night after your mother's ultimatum, and the next day, when I went in to work, I heard from Jules that Laura was gone. She'd snuck out, thankfully, in the night. Andy, you have to know I was prepared to talk her into leaving, walking away and leaving the babies, because I know what your mother's capable of. I know her family and have come face to face with her people. It's evil, and Laura and I will never win against that kind of power. It was weak of me to go down that road, and I hope you'll forgive me.

"Andy, I know you'll think me cowardly when you hear the news, but don't judge me too harshly. I can't go back to that cell. I survived it once. I wouldn't survive it at my age. This is better. Tell Laura I love her. I like to think she's my daughter, but she's not. You need to protect her and Gabriel, and I know I'm not wrong about you. There is something so strong in you that believes in right and wrong. Others may not see it, but I've seen what sets you apart from your family. I think from what you heard that you should know your mother may never stop trying to rid Laura from your life. Bless you, Andy, for having the courage to stand up for your family."

There was a rustling, and then there was nothing but static.

The phone rang, and Andy jumped and answered it before it could wake Laura. "Andy Friessen," he said.

"Mister Friessen, this is Stan Richards from the coroner's office. I was given your number by the sheriff. I'm calling on..." There was a rustling of papers.

Andy gritted his teeth and almost yelled through the phone that the man should show Aida some respect. "You're calling about Aida."

"Ah, yes, here it is Aida." The man cleared his throat roughly. "The cause of death has just been ruled a suicide. There was an overdose of Lunesta, a generic form of a sleeping pill, found in her system, enough to put down a horse. So there is no mistake that it wasn't an accident."

Andy swallowed and squeezed his eyes shut. "I see. Thank you for letting me know. Can you tell me when I can collect her remains? She has no family, and I'll be taking care of the arrangements."

There was a brief silence on the other end and then more rustling of papers. "We'll most likely be done tomorrow. The coroner just has to sign off on a few reports and she'll be ready to go. We'll call you and find out which funeral home you want her sent over to."

Andy held the disconnected phone and then set it down. He picked up the now silent recorder and stuffed it back in the envelope with the paper. Andy folded it over and then stepped into the living room, flicking off the kitchen light. He made a point of locking the front door, checking the deadbolt, the locks on the windows. It was something he had never done at the estate. It was always handled by the staff.

Andy wandered into the den at the back of the house beside the laundry room and the old desk pushed against the wall. He slid the top drawer open, shoved the envelope in back, and closed it. Andy leaned his hands on the desk, feeling dirty and dark, at a loss of what to do.

What he did have, he realized, with the tape and the note, was better than a smoking gun, for if something happened to Laura, he'd use this to blow his mother's world apart. Tomorrow, he'd take it to a safety deposit box and hope the day would never come that he'd have to use it.

Andy flicked the lights off in each room and walked up

the steps, stopping outside of Gabriel's room and then to look at his babies. They were sleeping soundly as if they knew he was their father, there to protect them. When he stepped into his bedroom with his wife, who was sleeping so soundly that she seemed like an angel, his angel, in his bed, he knew how right Aida had been. He'd never allow anything or anyone to threaten his family, his peace, and what was his: Laura, his wife; Gabriel, his son; Jeremy and Chelsea, his babies; the newest Friessens to this tiny corner of North Lakewood. It was the beginning of their brand new life together.

Turn the page for a sneak peek of
THE UNEXPECTED STORM the next book in *THE OUTSIDER SERIES*
Available in print, eBook and audio

—*"You can't help but fall in love with Neil and Candy. Neil is Candy's knight in shining armor"*

REVIEWER – APRIL

—*"It is nice to know that a story can be so powerful that a man can consider a woman's feelings and show her that love can conquer all and be lover's and friends"*

REVIEWER – THERESA

He can have any woman, except the one he wants.

In THE UNEXPECTED STORM, Candy McRae is
barely making ends meet. She's heartbroken and alone
with her horses and baby donkey living hand to mouth on
the most sought after oceanfront property. Everyone wants
it, including the wealthy hunk who owns the estate next
door. And when he offers to buy it she refuses. His first
mistake was asking her out. His second was not meaning it.
Even though he could solve all her problems, she'd rather
sell to the devil himself.

Smart and sexy Neil Friessen is quite the catch. He's not
only drop dead gorgeous with a body women dream of.
He's wealthy, stubborn, arrogant and thoughtful. He
attracts women, and million dollar deals, and plans to build
a resort on the property next to his. He has the plans, the
money, and the resources. The only thing standing
between him and his sweet deal is the dark haired beauty
who owns the property he wants.

When a storm forces everyone to evacuate Candy refuses
to leave her animals, and her property. But it's Neil who
shows up, Neil who rescues her. Except by the time he finds
her, vulnerable and hurt, they can't get out. Neil is alone
with the one woman he's always wanted. And he'll have to
choose between this dark haired beauty that fills his dreams
every night, and building his million dollar resort.

Chapter 1

Every once in a while, your heart has a mind of its own. It aches, it weeps, but there are days it soars and pumps with so much joy that you want to shout out to everyone just how wonderful everything is: The sun is perfect, the stars have all lined up, and you feel absolutely mind-blowingly freaking fantastic. The heart can also be responsible for you doing the most stupid, dumb-ass things ever, such as sliding your arms around the first good-looking babe you see and leaning in to taste her sweet lips with an out-of-this-world kiss that zings rockets right through your body, blowing off the top of your head, further proving you've checked your brain in to the nearest broom closet.

Maybe that was why Neil Friessen was standing barefoot, his shirt wide open, with the stinging outline of the sexiest hand imprinted on his face, after being slapped by the dark-haired babe he'd just kissed. She was drop-dead gorgeous, even with those smoky brown eyes sizzling with the fires of hell and shooting sparks his way. She had the most stunning set of long dark lashes, full rosy lips, a narrow nose, cheekbones that shaped her oval face, and a strong jaw. My God, this woman had him, Neil Friessen, a tall, "smart and sexy"—the exact words his sister-in-law Diana had used to describe him—man taking a nosedive in the dirt like some fumbling twenty-year-old. And Neil was definitely not fumbling or twenty.

Neil always had women hitting on him anywhere he went, and he loved it. It stoked his ego and made him feel damn good, not to mention he loved the ladies, especially those with mile-long legs and thick dark hair that had that bedroom look, as if he'd just run his fingers through those luscious locks. That was the babe standing before him on the sandy banks of the Atlantic Ocean, about thirty miles northwest of Cancun on the Yucatan Peninsula, where the forest met the ocean and where her horse, a beautiful smoky gray Azteca gelding, was ground tied on the sandy beach.

It wasn't as if he didn't know who she was: Candy McCrae, the daughter of Randy McCrae. Her father had bought this spectacular piece of paradise, two hundred acres of beach and rainforest, a property Neil had been trying to get his hands on for five years. The property backed onto the ten-thousand-acre parcel that Neil owned with his father, Rodney, and it was the missing key to their own paradise, the exact spot where Neil planned to build his five-star resort.

"Just what was that?" she spit out, and he could see the way she struggled to breathe, as if she'd just gone three rounds in a fight.

"Sorry. Lost my head is all, Candy. My brother Jed and his wife had a baby. Just got the news." Neil held up his cell phone as if to show her he was telling the truth.

She didn't cry or yell. What she did was fist her hands as if she was going to come at him again and pop him in the mouth this time, not that he didn't deserve it. But, hell, he'd wanted to kiss Candy as far back as he could remember. The trouble was that she hated him. No, it wasn't hate —it was the fact that she wished he'd die some horrible, painful death. He was pretty sure those had been her exact words when he asked her out for dinner two years ago and then a second time when he saw her in Cancun, getting supplies, eight months ago. That time, she had added in the "Drop dead" look she'd mastered just for him, and she did so every time since he tried to talk to her.

"Let me get this straight. Because you get news of something great happening in your life, your family, it gives you the right to trespass on my property, sneak up behind me, grab me, and kiss me. Or is there something else you're planning to do to ruin my life?" she snapped.

Her words were the second slap Neil had gotten in the past five minutes, and then it hit him: the vile, disgusting realization that she thought he, Neil Friessen, who could have any woman he wanted, was trying to force himself on her.

Hell, no! It was the first time he actually stuttered and backed up, waving his hands in front of him. "No, no, I don't think so. You got this all wrong, Candy." Then he rammed his fingers through his thick brown hair and took another step back. "Look, Candy, I am sorry. I just saw you sitting there...." Had he lost his mind? He almost said he'd wanted to taste her lips and take them for a test drive for as far back as he could remember. She'd looked so lost and innocent, sitting there in the sand, when he stepped over the dune and saw her. "Well, you stood up, and when you turned to face me, you had a look on your face as if you wanted me to kiss you. I kind of lost my head."

Neil didn't think she could get any angrier, but he was wrong. Her mouth gaped, and she appeared to lean closer, as if she was getting ready to blast him. Then she shut her mouth and crossed her arms tightly to her chest, tapping her foot.

"I was excited, and, my God, you were just there...."

"So you thought you could, what, have some fun with me? A romp in the sand and then send me on my way?" She gave him her back and stormed toward her horse, a few yards away.

"No, Candy, wait. I was actually on my way over to talk to you when I got this call. Look, I'm sorry." This was not going well. Neil was a master at working people, wooing women, and getting what he wanted. He'd always had a silver tongue, and he knew just the right thing to say and the perfect time to say it. He could always make everyone feel good about themselves, even when life dumped shit all around him. He saw the good in everything, including this feisty broad who stared at him as if he were a disease she had no intention of catching. Neil's sharp-witted tongue and nimble mind, which he counted on to talk him out of this mess with Candy, were, for the first time in his life, blank.

"Look, I want to talk to you about your property. I heard you went to Francisco Kan and asked him for help, offered him part ownership of your land, your property here." Neil swept his hand out in a dramatic gesture, but she stopped and spun around, planting both fists on her slim, sexy hips, which were exactly where his eyes went. She wore light khaki pants with a drawstring tie and a short sleeveless tee that showed her belly button and pale, flat abs.

"What? How the hell would you know anything about that?" She smacked her hand to her forehead as if she had realized something. "Why, that son of a bitch! Just what the hell did Francisco do, go running to you after he turned me down?"

"Is that what he did, turn you down?" Neil couldn't believe she wouldn't have come to him. When she didn't answer him, instead staring at him in a way that let him know she had shut down, he was certain something more was going on. He knew she struggled, and he didn't know how she made ends meet. When Francisco, a short, dark-haired Mayan in his late fifties, had come to him that morning and mentioned in his very calm way, without disclosing whatever it was that Candy was trying to hide, that she had come to him to ask him to invest in her property, well, Neil had decided to go and see Candy.

He should have known better, except he couldn't help worrying about her. He cared, even though she'd kicked him in the nuts one time after another, and he couldn't figure out what he'd done that had her loathing him. It bothered him, and he'd lost sleep over it, because she was the one woman who could push every single one of his buttons, turning bubbly and sharp-witted Neil Friessen into a raving lunatic.

"Look, I just want to talk to you. Would you come back here?"

"What do you want?" She made no move toward him. In fact, he could see every muscle in her arm tighten, and if he dared to step any closer to her, she'd probably deck him again.

"Candy, I've made you several generous offers to buy your property, and you've turned me down each time. If you're looking for a partner, I'd love to sit down with you and discuss it...."

"Oh, I just bet you would." She cut him off, grinding her teeth and spitting out each word. "Well, let me tell you something, Neil Friessen: I don't want you as a partner. I would rather go into business with the devil himself than have anything to do with the likes of you. Now get the hell off my property." She jabbed her finger angrily to the tree line and the path he'd taken to walk there.

"What the hell did I ever do to you, Candy? I can't for the love of God figure you out, woman," Neil barked. As he scrambled to think, he was sure he'd never done anything inappropriate. He liked her, he wanted to date her, and she fascinated him.

Candy narrowed those smoldering eyes, and this time he knew he'd get blasted. "You are a piece of work, Neil Friessen. You destroy people, you buy people, and you walk all over them if you don't get what you want. You use them and toss them away as if they're nothing, but you won't ever get that chance with me."

Candy stomped toward her horse, picking up the lead rope and looping it around his neck. His long mane appeared freshly brushed, and Neil wondered why she never trimmed it. They were both wild in a beautiful, mesmerizing way, completely in sync with each other, reading and anticipating one another's movements. He could actually picture the feeling of love between them. She mounted easily, riding bareback, and then turned her horse, staring down at Neil with the same blazing anger. It was so intense that even her horse sidestepped and pranced.

"If I find you on my property again, I'll shoot you." She kicked her horse and took off in a canter down the sandy beach to where her small two-bedroom home had been built just inside the shelter of the trees.

Neil watched, completely dumbstruck by her. His unbuttoned cotton shirt rustled in the breeze, and he rubbed his hand over light brown chest hair, wondering what the hell she thought he'd done. He spit on the ground. "Well, good riddance."

He was so done. He had come over here to offer his help, and she had practically spit on him again. Well, no more. He was so over her. He wasn't a masochist, so why did he keep acting as if he were? It was time he moved on and stopped thinking about her and allowing his guts to get so knotted up over her. He'd date other women, sure one of the two dozen women who'd been flirting with him for months would distract him. At least they appreciated who he was and what he had to offer. He was a fine catch, and he just knew one of them would interest him. Tonight would be the first night of the rest of his life.

CANDY SPURRED HER HORSE ON. "Come on, Sable!" she shouted. She leaned forward, racing over the thick white sand. The salty air mixed with the sound of the waves crashing against the shore, and she wanted to run and run. Her horse was responding, flying along with her. "Whoa, easy, boy." She sat heavier to slow the horse until he walked, and he snorted, breathing heavily just like she was.

They were completely in sync, understanding each other, her and her beautiful gray horse. He had reacted to her jolt of anger at Neil Friessen, her fury, her rage, and she knew better than to allow her blood to boil and her every emotion to spin out of control around her horse.

Being around Neil was an emotional roller coaster. She wanted to hate him, but every time she saw him, his presence shot fire right through her. She tried to tell herself it was because he was the best-looking man in these parts. Attraction and sexuality oozed out of him in a boy-next-door, best-friend kind of way. He had silky short brown hair and a strong, powerful face that reminded her of all those hot movie stars, but his eyes were the color of whiskey, endless, always dancing with a spark of light. Every time she saw him, she couldn't shake the image of him looking down on her in bed, and then she'd be furious at herself for going down that road—even though he had a body she'd love to explore, with tight abs and pecs under shirts that fit tastefully against his biceps. Lord, with those broad shoulders, it was clear the man worked out, but he probably owned some fancy home gym with a personal trainer and all.

She pulled up to the corral where she kept her horses and slid off Sables' back, hitting the ground. He was sixteen hands high, a big boy, all solid muscle, but he was sweet and loyal, and he always knew what she was thinking. He nuzzled her cheek, and she kissed his muzzle and patted his shoulder before loosely tying him to the corral fence.

As she brushed her horse down softly, she had to remind herself that Neil Friessen was just playing with her, and it hurt like hell. She wanted to be loved, not toyed with, and she knew the only reason he was nice to her and was pursuing her, all flirty and interested, was because he wanted her land. The first time he asked her out, her dad had still been alive, and he warned her that they were sitting on prime real estate and that the Friessens wanted their property. Going out with Neil would only get her heart broken, because he had an agenda. Her dad had said that Neil would do anything to get their property, even pretend an interest in Candy. She'd listened thankfully, even though it stung beyond belief, because she wanted his interest to be genuine. The last time she saw Neil, he'd just finished with some blonde, carrying her bag and setting it in a cab, hugging her. Then he'd spotted Candy. Candy had been stunned, because she couldn't believe he had the gall to ask her on a date less than five minutes after he'd been with another woman. Although she was proud of what she'd said, telling him to drop dead, she really wanted to hate him. It would be easier, and her heart would stop flip-flopping from her toes to her head every time she saw him. Even today she'd been embarrassed by how much she wanted that kiss, which was why she'd slapped him as hard as she could. She had known he was there, striding behind her, and when she stood up, her heart had flipped a switch, as if lightning zinged through her when his lips touched hers.

She touched her swollen lips, still burning, and licked the taste of Neil from them. It was so much like the sweetest dessert she anticipated and loved, and she wanted seconds. But she couldn't have firsts, and she couldn't have seconds, so she watched her horse prancing in the corral with her two other horses, a dark thoroughbred and a palomino, and she focused on her problems, wondering what she'd have to sell next to buy their feed, to pay the farrier and the local vet. There, it had worked, and she felt like absolute crap.

About the Author

"Lorhainne Eckhart is one of my go to authors when I want a guaranteed good book. So many twists and turns, but also so much love and such a strong sense of family."

(LORA W., REVIEWER)

New York Times & USA Today bestseller Lorhainne Eckhart is best known for writing Raw Relatable Real Romance where "Morals and family are running themes." As one fan calls her, she is the "Queen of the family saga." (aherman) writing "the ups and downs of what goes on within a family but also with some suspense, angst and of course a bit of romance thrown in for good measure."

Follow Lorhainne on Bookbub to receive alerts on New Releases and Sales and join her mailing list at Lorhainne-Eckhart.com for her Monday Blog, all book news, giveaways and FREE reads. With over 120 books, audiobooks, and multiple series published and available at all, retailers now translated into six languages. She is a multiple recipient of the Readers' Favorite Award for Suspense and Romance, and lives in the Pacific Northwest on an island, is the mother of three, her oldest has autism and she is an advocate for never giving up on your dreams.

"Lorhainne Eckhart has this uncanny way of just hitting the spot every time with her books."

(CAROLINE L., REVIEWER)

The O'Connells: *The O'Connells of Livingston, Montana are not your typical family. A riveting collection of stories surrounding the ups and downs of what goes on within a family but also with some suspense, angst and of course a bit of romance thrown in for good measure. "I thought I loved the Friessens, but I absolutely adore the O'Connell's. Each and every book has different genres of stories, but the one thing in common is how she is able to wrap it around the family, which is the heart of each story." (C. Logue)*

The Friessens: *An emotional big family romance series, the Friessen family siblings find their relationships tested, lay their hearts on the line, and discover lasting love! "Lorhainne Eckhart is one of my go to authors when I want* *a guaranteed good book. So many twists and turns, but also so much love and such a strong sense of family."* (Lora W., Reviewer)

The Parker Sisters: *The Parker Sisters are a close-knit family, and like any other family they have their ups and downs. Eckhart has crafted another intense family drama… "The character development is outstanding, and the emotional investment is high…"* (Aherman, Reviewer)

The McCabe Brothers: *Join the five McCabe siblings on their journeys to the dark and dangerous side of love! An intense, exhilarating collection of romantic thrillers you won't want to miss. — "Eckhart has a new series that is definitely worth the read. The queen of the family saga started this series with a spin-off of her wildly successful Friessen series." From a Readers' Favorite award—winning author and "queen of the family saga"* (Aherman)

Lorhainne loves to hear from her readers! You can connect with me at:
www.LorhainneEckhart.com
lorhainneeckhart.le@gmail.com

Also by Lorhainne Eckhart

The Outsider Series
The Forgotten Child (Brad and Emily)
A Baby and a Wedding *(An Outsider Series Short)*
Fallen Hero (Andy, Jed, and Diana)
The Search *(An Outsider Series Short)*
The Awakening (Andy and Laura)
Secrets (Jed and Diana)
Runaway (Andy and Laura)
Overdue *(An Outsider Series Short)*
The Unexpected Storm (Neil and Candy)
The Wedding (Neil and Candy)

The Friessens: A New Beginning
The Deadline (Andy and Laura)
The Price to Love (Neil and Candy)
A Different Kind of Love (Brad and Emily)
A Vow of Love, A Friessen Family Christmas

The Friessens
The Reunion
The Bloodline (Andy & Laura)
The Promise (Diana & Jed)
The Business Plan (Neil & Candy)
The Decision (Brad & Emily)
First Love (Katy)
Family First
Leave the Light On
In the Moment
In the Family

In the Silence
In the Charm
Unexpected Consequences
It Was Always You
The First Time I Saw You
Welcome to My Arms
Welcome to Boston
I'll Always Love You
Ground Rules
A Reason to Breathe
You Are My Everything
Anything For You
The Homecoming
Stay Away From My Daughter
The Bad Boy
A Place of Our Own
The Visitor
All About Devon
Long Past Dawn
How to Heal a Heart
Keep Me In Your Heart

The O'Connells
The Neighbor
The Third Call
The Secret Husband
The Quiet Day
The Commitment
The Missing Father
The Hometown Hero
Justice
The Family Secret
The Fallen O'Connell
The Return of the O'Connells

And The She Was Gone
The Stalker
The O'Connell Family Christmas
The Girl Next Door
Broken Promises
The Gatekeeper
The Hunted

The McCabe Brothers

Don't Stop Me (Vic)
Don't Catch Me (Chase)
Don't Run From Me (Aaron)
Don't Hide From Me (Luc)
Don't Leave Me (Claudia)
Out of Time

A Billy Jo McCabe Mystery

Nothing As it Seems
Hiding in Plain Sight
The Cold Case
The Trap
Above the Law
The Stranger at the Door
The Children
The Last Stand
The Charity
The Sacrifice

The Street Fighter

Finding Home

The Wilde Brothers

The One (Joe and Margaret)
The Honeymoon, A Wilde Brothers Short

Friendly Fire (Logan and Julia)
Not Quite Married, A Wilde Brothers Short
A Matter of Trust (Ben and Carrie)
The Reckoning, A Wilde Brothers Christmas
Traded (Jake)
Unforgiven (Samuel)
The Holiday Bride

Married in Montana
His Promise
Love's Promise
A Promise of Forever

The Parker Sisters
Thrill of the Chase
The Dating Game
Play Hard to Get
What We Can't Have
Go Your Own Way
A June Wedding

Kate & Walker
One Night
Edge of Night
Last Night

Walk the Right Road Series
The Choice
Lost and Found
Merkaba
Bounty
Blown Away: The Final Chapter
He Came Back

The Saved Series
Saved
Vanished
Captured

Single Titles
Loving Christine

www.ingramcontent.com/pod-product-compliance
Lightning Source LLC
Chambersburg PA
CBHW030932210726
48290CB00007B/2164